Exploring the Chicago World's Fair

1893

Books by Laurie Lawlor

The Worm Club
How to Survive Third Grade
Addie Across the Prairie
Addie's Long Summer
Addie's Dakota Winter
George on His Own
Gold in the Hills
Little Women *(a movie novelization)*

Heartland series
Heartland: Come Away with Me
Heartland: Take to the Sky
Heartland: Luck Follows Me

American Sisters series
West Along the Wagon Road 1852
A *Titanic* Journey Across the Sea 1912
Voyage to a Free Land 1630
Adventure on the Wilderness Road 1775
Crossing the Colorado Rockies 1864
Down the Río Grande 1829
Horseback on the Boston Post Road 1704
Exploring the Chicago World's Fair 1893

American SISTERS

Exploring the Chicago World's Fair

1893

Laurie Lawlor

A MINSTREL® HARDCOVER
PUBLISHED BY POCKET BOOKS

New York   London   Toronto   Sydney   Singapore

A MINSTREL HARDCOVER

 A Minstrel Book published by
POCKET BOOKS, a division of Simon & Schuster, Inc.
1230 Avenue of the Americas, New York, NY 10020

ISBN: 0-671-03924-5

First Minstrel Books hardcover printing March 2001

10 9 8 7 6 5 4 3 2 1

A MINSTREL BOOK and colophon are registered trademarks
of Simon & Schuster, Inc.

Cover illustration by Ernie Norcia

Printed in the U.S.A.

For Kate

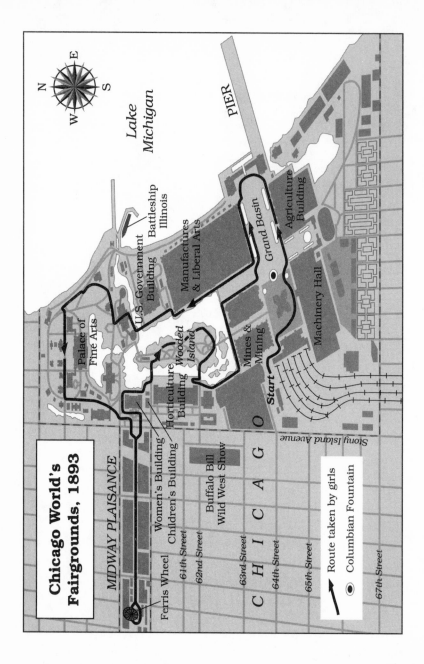

Chicago World's Fairgrounds, 1893

MIDWAY PLAISANCE

Ferris Wheel
Women's Building
Children's Building
Buffalo Bill
Wild West Show

Palace of
Fine Arts

Horticulture
Building

*Wooded
Island*

U.S. Government
Building

Battleship
Illinois

Manufactures
& Liberal Arts

Mines &
Mining

Grand Basin

Machinery Hall

Agriculture
Building

Start

PIER

*Lake
Michigan*

Stony Island Avenue

C H I C A G O

61st Street
62nd Street
63rd Street
64th Street
65th Street
67th Street

N
W E
S

→ Route taken by girls
● Columbian Fountain

Exploring the Chicago World's Fair

1893

Introduction

On May 1, 1893, the World's Columbian Exposition in Chicago, Illinois, opened for business. It was called the most famous fair ever held on American soil. In the next 179 days, the displays and exhibits from around the country and around the world would be visited by nearly 27 million people—a striking number considering the fact that the entire country at the time had a total population of just 63 million.

The fair was a landmark event, a once-in-a-lifetime experience for the 150,000 ordinary men, women, and children who visited the 600-acre site each day. Their responses were overwhelming and enthusiastic. "Sell the cook stove if necessary and come," writer Hamlin Garland told his aging parents in South Dakota. "You must see this fair!" It was reported that one woman from Texas was so determined to visit the fair that she walked 1,300 miles on railroad ties from Galveston, Texas, to Chicago.

Famous architects, planners, artists, and builders worked together to create a remarkable series of buildings, lagoons, parks, and boulevards where a swamp once stood. The White City, as the fair was nicknamed, became almost overnight a praised vision of what a perfect, civilized city could be — a place with clean streets, fresh drinking water, and no crime.

The fair was created only 22 years after downtown Chicago had been wiped out in a terrible fire and just five years after a terrorist's bomb had unleashed a bloody riot between strikers and police in Haymarket Square. Officially, Chicagoans claimed that the reason for the World's Columbian Exposition was to celebrate technological progress and the 400th anniversary of Columbus's discovery of North America. The real rationale had undoubtedly to do with Chicagoans' desire to prove to the rest of the world that their city had risen above strife, ashes, and chaos.

It was a remarkable vision staged under remarkable circumstances. The year that the fair opened, America's economy was racked by depression. Farmers were organizing mass protest movements. Workers were marching in the streets. And yet the fair symbolized unity, a kind of hopeful belief of Americans at the time that the nineteenth century was truly "the greatest era of civilized progress the world had ever seen."

Chapter 1

"Tell it again."

"Which part?"

"Everything."

Dora sighed. She had already told her three younger sisters the story one thousand times since they'd left the ranch in Saddlestring, Nebraska. As their eastbound train rumbled toward Chicago, she took a deep breath and leaned forward toward Lillian and Phoebe in the facing seat. "At the fair the buildings are white and splendid and big," Dora said. Expertly, she shifted four-year-old Tess, their sleeping youngest sister, in her lap. "The sidewalk moves by itself and a giant wheel carries people up into the sky. There's a real, genuine castle you can visit and—"

"What if we fall off?" ten-year-old Phoebe demanded nervously.

"Stop interrupting," Lillian said. She was eight and fearless. The Ferris wheel was her favorite. "Nobody falls because they're inside a car like this with walls and a ceiling."

"Oh," said Phoebe. She looked around at the sixty-five passengers jammed into grubby, hard seats on the rocking, rattling Union Pacific car. The hot, close air smelled of whisky, tobacco, and sweat. The ceiling drummed with the sound of cinders belched against the roof from the steam engine's smokestack. Across the aisle a baby wailed. A woman blew her nose loudly and shouted in a strange language at two wrestling boys. A man in a cowboy hat snored. Phoebe decided she'd skip the Ferris wheel.

"At the fair there are many inventions," Dora continued. "I don't know all the names. Electric machines and gadgets and—"

"You forgot to tell about the cheese," Phoebe said.

Dora rolled her eyes. "At the fair there is an eleven-ton cheese and a fifteen-hundred-pound chocolate statue of a beautiful woman named Venus and a real battleship and trained lions, tigers, and elephants and—"

Lillian smiled dreamily. "I'm going to have a little taste." She smacked her lips. "Just a nibble."

Phoebe scowled. "You mean a crumb of chocolate from her toe? You'll get in trouble."

"Nobody will notice. Venus is huge. She weighs tons," Lillian said indignantly. "Do you know how big that is?"

Phoebe shook her head. "Dora, how much is tons?"

Dora, who always impressed her sisters with her knowledge of nearly everything, wasn't listening. She was staring at the scuffed toes of her worn-out, too-small boots. What if all the other twelve-year-old girls in Chicago wore shiny, new shoes?

"Dora!" Phoebe insisted. "Lillian says she's going to steal chocolate. She's going to be arrested."

"I didn't say I'm going to *steal* Venus's toe. I just said I'm going to taste it," Lillian said angrily.

Dora looked at Lillian and Phoebe as if they were both crazy. "Can't you two get along for five minutes? If your shrieking wakes up Tess, you have to play with her," Dora warned. She looked down at her sleeping sister. Tess's matted hair smelled sour and dusty and had left a damp spot on Dora's skirt. Under one chubby arm Tess clutched beloved Nancy, a rag doll with black bead eyes and one arm missing.

"You forgot the camels and donkeys," Lillian complained.

Phoebe pouted. "You forgot the balloon ride and the volcano and the gold mine."

"I'll tell the rest later," Dora said and yawned. "Now leave me alone." She shut her eyes.

Bored, Phoebe sat up on her knees and pressed her sweaty face against the grimy train window. The mark she made on the glass looked like a ghost staring in at her and her three sisters. "See, Lillian?" she said proudly. She ran her finger along the outline of flattened nose, wide forehead, and shallow chin.

"Not as ugly as you in real life," Lillian replied without glancing up. Dainty Lillian was practicing her autograph with a stubby pencil and a paper scrap. Again and again she wrote the stage name she had invented: "LillianLucilleMariePomeroy" spelled all together so the whole name would have to be used and would take up as much room as possible on the marquee.

Phoebe frowned and wiped her greasy face mark from the window with her sleeve. She was dark haired like the other Pomeroy girls, but her lips were thin and her ears were overlarge. Mama called her too plain to go on stage professionally, which was fine with shy Phoebe, who did not like to sing or dance. Critically, Phoebe examined her dirty sleeve, which had now become even dirtier. Her eyes narrowed with anger. She gave pretty, irritating Lillian a swift, secret jab with her elbow.

"Ouch!" Lillian wailed.

"Sorry." Phoebe made a contrite little smile.

Dora's eyes flew open. "Stop it, both of you."

"Better not have given me a bruise," Lillian grumbled.

Phoebe stuck out her tongue.

Dora pretended not to notice. The train car bucked and rattled. She wished she could open the window, that there'd be a fresh, cool breeze—not more dust rolling from across the plains or more cinders blown in from the smokestack. Her eyelids lowered. Her head drifted against the sooty window frame.

Carefully, Phoebe removed a battered penny postcard from her pocket. "Let me borrow your pencil, Lillian," she whispered.

"What for?" Lillian demanded. She held the pencil tightly in her fist.

"I told Florence I'd write her."

Lillian puckered her mouth. "Next thing you'll be asking for a penny to mail it. Well, don't bother, because I'm saving my money for the Ferris wheel."

"Just for a minute," Phoebe pleaded. "Come on, Lillian."

At the sound of Phoebe's familiar, high-pitched

whine, Dora opened one eye. "Give her the pencil, Lillian. Stop being so stingy for once."

Lillian made a great puffing noise. "Don't use it all up. And don't go biting the wood. I don't like teeth marks on my only pencil." Reluctantly, she handed Phoebe the pencil.

"Thank you," Phoebe replied and made a nasty face. Cleverly, she positioned the postcard in her lap with one arm wrapped around it so that Lillian, sitting beside her, could not see what she was struggling to write:

Deeer Florence:
Never got too say good by to you
Papa said we got to skip out at nite
for the sherriff comes I will trie to send
you a reel souveneer post card from the FAIR
do not ever forget your old frend—Phoebe

"Done?" Lillian demanded with her palm outstretched.

Phoebe handed back the pencil. "That's all the words I can fit." She slid the postcard back into her pocket.

Dora stretched her arms over her head. Her leg was cramping under Tess's weight. She felt as if they had been traveling for days.

"How far till Chicago?" Lillian demanded.

"Supposed to be there this evening," Dora said. She stared out the window. Dry, gray-green Iowa blurred past. Dark clouds herded against the horizon, which stretched like a taut line of barbed wire.

"I liked the ranch," Phoebe said in a quiet voice to no one in particular. "First place we ever lived three years in a row. Our first real house." She sighed. "We even had curtains."

Lillian drummed her fingers on the worn, red upholstery. "I'm glad we're going to a big city with lots of bright lights. We're going to see the fair. And don't forget the Wild West Show. We're going to be famous this time, just like Mama said. The ranch was dull. Exactly the same every day."

Dora turned and glanced over her shoulder at their mother dozing in the seat behind them. No one would have guessed that the woman in the yellow taffeta silk skirt and knobby broadcloth cape with most of the pearl buttons missing was once a ranch wife in a faded gingham apron. On her lap she clutched her precious, well-traveled hatbox. Her chin had dropped to her chest, and the fake bluebird on her gayest fancy straw hat bobbed and leapt as if trying to free itself as the train lurched along.

Dora remembered a meadowlark she had once found caught by one wing on a fence on her way to school. The bird's beating heart, bones, and feathers had felt light as wind when she'd let it go. Did the meadowlark remember her? She turned and stared out the window. "No more school," she said in a soft, mournful voice.

Phoebe nodded sadly. "No more friends."

"You'll make new ones," Lillian replied with impatience. "And what was so wonderful about Miss Elvira Simpson and that schoolhouse with the rattlesnakes under the floorboards and those nasty boys lurking around at recess? I hated school. I'm glad we don't have to go no more."

"Any more," Dora corrected her.

"That's what I said," Lillian replied. Her pretty face flushed bright red. "Sometimes I think you two are the dullest creatures on earth. Dora, you with your stupid spelling bee awards and you, Phoebe, with your stupid Wards Catalog."

Phoebe frowned. "Wards Catalog isn't stupid. It's beautiful."

Lillian sensed that she had hit her mark. "You're probably the only ten-year-old girl in all of Nebraska who studied the stupid advertisements and cut out the stupid pictures of stoves and tables and chairs and sewing machines—"

"That's enough," Dora said. She could see that Phoebe was blinking hard and biting both her lips at once. To cry would signal complete defeat— something Lillian would never let Phoebe forget. "Don't fight. We need to stick together. That's what Papa said, remember?"

Lillian folded her arms in front of herself and flounced backward against the hard seat. Phoebe ran her fingers down a pleat of her patched serge skirt. Dora tried not to feel angry about Lillian's comment about Miss Simpson and the spelling bees. Dora was proud of how well she could spell hard words like *incinerate* and *parallel.* She liked school. She liked doing something besides taking care of her younger sisters.

School was escape. When she went to school she could practice writing perfectly shaped vowels with elegant wiggly tails, and wash the blackboard better than anyone, and read difficult words no one else could pronounce from the McGuffey's Reader. And best of all, Miss Simpson praised her. Dora was special at school. At home she was just somebody who cooked and swept and did laundry. She had to wipe dirty noses and bandage bloody knees and make up games to keep her sisters from killing each other. School was easy. Everything else in Dora's life was hard. Everything.

"Wanna lemonade," Tess said, awake now. She sat up and rubbed her grubby fists in her large blue eyes. She stared hard at the boy across the aisle, who was sipping something from a glass bottle beaded with moisture.

"Hush," Dora replied. "We don't have any money."

"Wanna lemonade," Tess repeated, more insistent this time.

"Take her for some water, will you, Lillian?" Dora asked.

"Why me?" Lillian demanded. The doll Nancy tumbled from Tess's arms and landed upside down on the seat. "Come on, Little Kisses," Lillian said, using Tess's nickname. Lillian took her thirsty sister by the hand and dragged her down the aisle toward the water spigot, which dribbled warm, rusty-tasting water into a paper-tasting cone.

As soon as Lillian and Tess disappeared, Phoebe asked quietly, "Dora, do you think Wards Catalog is stupid?"

"No, of course not."

Phoebe examined her ragged fingernails. "You think I'm ugly?"

"No, I do not. You shouldn't pay so much attention to Lillian. You know how she goes on and on sometimes just to hear the sound of her own voice. She doesn't mean half what she says."

Phoebe's thin shoulders seemed to relax. She spread her fingers out on her lap. "Twenty times. We moved twenty times in ten years. I counted. You think we'll stay put in Chicago?"

Dora shrugged. She didn't want to give her worried sister false hope. Papa had what he called a natural disposition to remove to a new country. It was in his blood, he said. His papa and his papa's papa did the same. "Pomeroys never settle down," he liked to brag. Like his ancestors, Papa did not need much reason to move on, to pull up roots and head out for some distant, better opportunity. Dora's family's life was rooted in rootlessness. Sometimes it seemed to her as if they'd played every little run-down theater and two-bit circus act between New Jersey and California, crisscrossing the country from one small town to the next mining camp and back again. In all those years, Dora had been to school only a total of four years.

"Girls!" Mama gave Dora's shoulder a poke. "Will you look out that window? Before you know it we'll be crossing the Mississippi. Oh, I can tell you I can hardly wait to be in a big city again. Chicago! You never saw anything so beautiful in all your life."

Dora twisted in her seat to catch a glimpse of

Mama fanning herself with her slender, gloved hand as she bent over the red-faced man sitting next to her, beside the window. "Excuse me, sir, but I just have to keep looking for Illinois," Mama apologized in her sweetest melted butter voice.

Unlike Dora, who had dry, frizzy dark hair, Mama's hair was thick and auburn. Mama's eyes were dark and striking and she had high cheek-bones, which she said helped her "light up on stage." Dora always knew there was something slightly exotic about Mama's beauty, yet this after-noon she felt as if she were looking at a stranger. That was when she realized what had changed. Her mother was smiling. She had not seen her mother look so happy in years.

"Going home, ma'am?" the stranger asked and pushed his stained, felt hat back on his meaty fore-head.

"You might say we're going to our *real* home. The stage. We've been away awhile. Maybe you've heard of the Magnificent Pomeroy Performers and Their Talking Horse?"

The stranger shook his head. Phoebe blushed. Dora wished her mother would speak in a more quiet voice. What if everyone on the train car was listening?

"Well, if you missed our act, maybe you saw me

in *Uncle Tom's Cabin* or maybe *The Count of Monte Cristo.*"

The man's silence seemed to indicate he was stumped.

Mama did not give up so easily. "I did *Ten Nights in a Barroom* at the Belmont before it burned. A very popular show."

"I seen that! That was good," he gushed.

Mama smiled and fingered one of the velvet rosettes on her hat brim. "Of course that was ages ago. Before all four girls were born. We're starting a new routine. Calling it Barn Yard Musicians. Chicken imitations, dogs jumping through fiery hoops, that kind of thing. I'm quite a dancer and, of course, so are my precious little daughters. I have four daughters, sir. Each one more talented than the next. We had a nice act. Of course, that was before we took up ranching. Hated it. Absolutely hated it. Nothing worse than eleven months of wind and winter in Nebraska. After the bank foreclosed we decided to head to Chicago. Like everybody else, I guess," she said. Her nervous laughter sounded musical.

The stranger smiled. One of his front teeth was missing.

"I'm sure you've heard of the Wild West Show and Buffalo Bill?"

The stranger nodded eagerly.

"My husband," Mama said with a dramatic pause, "has been hired by Buffalo Bill himself to be one of the horse handlers. He was a trick rider before he hurt his back. A real professional daredevil."

Dora and her sister shrank lower and lower into their seats as if somehow they could become invisible.

"Well Buffalo Bill, Bill, as we like to call him," Mama continued, "he heard about my husband and he hired him on the spot. Of course I'm going to audition. Maybe get my babies on stage, too. Ever been to Chicago?"

"Sure. Sure—"

"We're going to be right across the street from the World's Columbian Exposition. We're going to be performing for thousands of folks every day."

"The fair! Now there's something," the stranger managed to interrupt Mama. "Unbelievable. The chance of a lifetime. Why I've heard—"

Before he could get another word in edgewise, Mama burst into a long monologue about their costumes and their songs and their unfortunate contract in San Francisco and how the trick horse died halfway across Nevada, which was one reason they ended up in Nebraska and she was certainly glad to be getting back to civilization again. She bet he was glad, too, wasn't he?

"Yes, ma'am," the stranger said with some confusion. He seemed grateful when the train pulled into a water stop for the engine. He stood up and tipped his hat and took a long walk out to the platform.

Dora twisted in her seat. "Do you have to talk so loud to strangers, Mama?" she hissed.

Mama patted her face with a handkerchief and checked her hair, using a small mirror from her cheap square pocketbook, which was made of embossed leather and was worn white around the ball catch. "Dora," she said, looking with disdain over the top of the mirror. "Never, never underestimate the effect of a little advance publicity." She dropped the mirror in the purse and snapped it shut. "Where's your father?"

"Haven't seen him since Omaha," replied Phoebe, who, like the rest of her sisters, knew very well where Papa had gone. Phoebe didn't want to tell Mama for fear of a scene. Besides, she was enjoying Mama's rare good mood.

Mama arranged her cape and glanced cheerfully up and down the car, which was emptying of the crowd of ragged families, limping cowboys, and down-on-their-luck salesmen traveling on the cheapest fares possible. "Do you think all these people are out of work?"

Dora shrugged. It was unusual for Mama to think about other people's circumstances. How many times had she reminded Dora and her sisters that other people's troubles were just too depressing? She had enough problems of her own, she liked to say, to worry about anybody else.

Mama peered happily out the window and sang in a soft voice:

"Then come sit by my side if you love me;
Do not hasten to bid me adieu.
But remember the Red River Valley
and the cowboy that loved you so true . . ."

The familiar tune made Dora smile at Phoebe. Neither girl had heard their mother sing "Red River Valley" in a long, long time. "Remember?" Phoebe whispered to her sister.

"Haven't heard it since before the El Grande Theater in Leadville," Dora replied. She smiled. Maybe everything was going to work out fine after all. Maybe Chicago and the Wild West Show would be their lucky break.

The train whistle wailed. "All aboard!" the conductor shouted.

Dora glanced at Nancy, sprawled in the seat

across from them. She jumped to her feet. "What's wrong?" Phoebe demanded.

"Tess and Lillian! Where are they?" Dora said. Desperately, she pushed her way up the aisle through the crowd of passengers piling back on the train again. What if her sisters had wandered off the train onto the platform?

"Tess, Lillian!" she called in desperation.

"Last call! All aboard!" the conductor called. A bell rang.

Dora looked out over the empty platform. What if they'd been kidnapped? She was about to alert the conductor when she heard a familiar giggle. Tess and Lillian stood in the passageway between the two train cars. They carried bottles in their arms. "Where'd you get that lemonade?" Dora demanded, angry and relieved at the same time.

"Lillian," Tess said sweetly.

Dora shot a suspicious glance at her grinning sister.

"Train boy was selling them and he said he had some extras," Lillian explained. "Little Kisses was so thirsty. Got one for you and Phoebe, too. Can't call me stingy now, can you?"

Chapter

2

They smelled Chicago before they saw it. Early the next morning, after innumerable stops and starts and breakdowns and switching on and off the tracks all night long, the Chicago and Northwestern caromed across the Fox River. By the time they reached the city limits, an unseasonably hot June breeze was blowing from the southeast. The strong stench filled Dora and her sisters' noses and made them gasp. Experienced train passengers who had visited Chicago before automatically held handkerchiefs to their faces.

"What's that awful stink?" Dora asked Mama.

Mama couldn't answer. She held her handkerchief to her mouth and nose and blinked.

"Union Stock Yards," proudly answered the

red-faced stranger next to Mama. "That's where they butcher thirteen thousand hogs every day. A real tourist attraction. Ought to see it while you're here."

Lillian groaned. She had had enough of the smell of manure and cattle on the ranch.

"Can't see a thing," Phoebe said with disappointment. She stared hard out the window, which was enveloped with gray smoke. Phoebe and the other girls kept looking, waiting for a glimpse of their family's salvation. Dora worried. Maybe their parents had been wrong. Maybe Chicago wasn't paradise.

"Chicago! End of the line! Transfers east, south, and north must get off the train!" the conductor shouted. "Claim your baggage at the platform."

The chuffing, huffing train ground to a halt. The engine rumbled low, like a bull pawing the dirt, so that the train car floor continued to vibrate with a dull roar. Mama stood and adjusted her hat. She held tight to her hatbox with one arm. "Chicago!" she exclaimed as if they had just reached the Promised Land.

Weary, soiled passengers clambered for their baskets and babies and bags and streamed out of their seats and down the aisle like melted snow water. For a moment, Dora spotted what she thought was Da at the front of the train car. She knew that brilliant flash of teeth anywhere. He waved.

"Da!" Dora called.

The crowd swallowed him up in noise and confusion.

"You see your father?" Mama demanded.

Dora nodded and pointed toward the front of the car. "He went that way."

"Come on, girls," Mama said. "We'll meet your father outside. Dora, you carry Tess. Come on, Phoebe and Lillian. Hold tight to each other and walk toward the rear of the train."

Dora hitched her sticky, hungry sister on one hip. She stepped off the train and onto the platform and entered the swirling current of elbowing passengers. The heartless crush and bustle and shove of the depot overwhelmed her. Desperately, she tried to keep one eye on her two sisters, who drifted ahead, bobbed like driftwood, and vanished in the wrong direction. Everyone was being pushed by a look-alike sea of dark-suited arms and legs and hats. A million women carried the same umbrella and carpetbag valise and wore the same tippy hat with ribbons and feathers. Where had all these people come from? Where were they all going?

"Phoebe! Lillian!" Dora screamed and trailed after them. Tess held her hands to her ears to block the deafening clang and hiss and boom of the terrifying black locomotive, which dripped and squealed and writhed in smoke. She hid her face from the evil, glistening wheels that seemed to tower over her and her sister. To keep Nancy safe, Tess bit her doll's one good arm with all her might so that the engine monster could not grab away Nancy and crush her.

The relentless crowd moved like an angry river at flood stage. Dora struggled along with her little sister in her arms. She wriggled past a fat woman carrying a yapping dog, past a man with a basket of apples. She jumped up and down, but she was still too short. Everything blocked her view. Where were her sisters? She could not spot either Phoebe or Lillian. She might never find them again.

"Dora!" Da boomed in his loudest, best theatrical voice.

Dora turned. She couldn't see him, but she could hear him somewhere behind her. She turned and tried swimming against the swarming crowd. As she did, she was nearly sucked into the undertow of passengers following a sweaty baggage handler who toted a trunk on one shoulder. For a second she thought she caught a glimpse of Phoebe's white dress. She shouldered her way closer, darted, dodged, reached and hooked a handful of fabric. "Phoebe!" she screamed. To Dora's amazement, Phoebe had held tight to Lillian. The four girls stood together, a shivering island in the midst of a seething surf of bewildered, bellowing passengers.

Lillian quickly took control of the situation. "Link up!" she ordered over the din of voices and metallic shrieks and hissing steam. Her sisters joined elbows. "Where's Mama?"

"Don't know," Dora spoke as loudly as she could into her sister's ear. "I heard Da's voice. We should stay put so he can find us."

Dora and her sisters hobbled their way close to a gritty steel column, which seemed like the most stationary place they could anchor themselves. A train whistle pierced the air. The crowd seemed to be draining away. "Hold Tess up," Phoebe suggested. "Maybe she can spot Mama or Da."

"Look for Mama's hat," Dora told Tess and lifted her as high as she could. Excitedly, Tess took Nancy from her mouth and pointed. But when her sisters jumped and strained to see who was coming, they discovered just another woman in another hat with a bird.

"We'll never find our parents," Phoebe wailed. "We'll have to stay in this train station forever."

"Shut up," Lillian said. "Keep looking. They've got to get the trunk. They can't leave without that."

"What about us?" Phoebe said. "They might leave without us."

Suddenly, Dora spied Mama, hat askew. Mama determinedly shoved her way toward them, using the hatbox as a kind of shield. "Where's your father?" she demanded.

"Heard him just for a moment," Dora said. "He disappeared."

Little by little, the crowd began to thin out. For the first time, it was possible to look around and see more than the steady wave of moving passengers. "Baggage car. We'll try the baggage car," Mama said. "This way."

Like ducklings swimming upstream behind their mother, Dora and her sisters followed Mama. The baggage car was easier to locate than Dora had thought. They had simply to follow the sound of crashing and cursing.

"Look out!" the baggage handlers shouted from the open freight car. One by one trunks and boxes and valises flew through the air and landed on the platform with jarring thuds and splintering crashes.

"Will you, sir, be careful with that trunk!" a woman called.

The baggage handlers paid her no mind. They tossed each piece of luggage with equal disrespect and ferocity. "Earl!" Mama shouted and stood her ground. "Earl Pomeroy!"

Da turned, removed his battered derby, and revealed his big, close-cropped head. He waved his hat in the air. He was a stocky man with a platinum blond moustache and a chiseled small mouth that broke into a glittering grin. "There you are, my lovelies!" he called.

The sound of his familiar, confident voice filled Dora with relief. Now they were safe. They had found Da. For one moment, Dora felt boneless, as if all the strength had oozed out of her bruised arms. Her little sister seemed indescribably heavy.

"Where have you been, Earl Pomeroy?" Mama demanded angrily. "You abandoned us on the train for hours and then we were nearly crushed to death trying to find you in the depot."

"So sorry, my sweet. I met up with some old acquaintances in the next car," Da said. He avoided Mama's steely gaze by concentrating on the baggage flying through the air.

Mama breathed hard through her nose. "I knew it. You said you wouldn't. You promised."

"Just a couple hands of euchre. Nothing big. Just nickels." He smiled his charming smile, shoved his hand in his pocket, and made a jingling noise.

Mama's eyes narrowed. "You promised. No more cards. No more gambling."

"So I did, my sweet. And now that we've arrived in this fair city, I vow to be faithful to my promise." He gave Mama a loud kiss on the cheek.

Mama drew back. She tilted her head and studied him carefully. "I hope you still have the paper Cody gave you with the address where we're supposed to stay. Didn't gamble that away, too, did you?"

Da nodded and patted his coat pocket. "Right here safe and sound. Never fear. Chicago is a new start, my sweet. I'm turning over a new leaf," he promised. When he turned and saw his four daughters observing him, he looked startled for a split second. His nervous, sky-colored eyes scanned each witness. Then he quickly regained his composure. "Well, my lovelies," he said with great enthusiasm, "what do you think about Chicago?"

"Stinks," Tess said and held her nose.

Da laughed loudly. He gave her fat cheek an affectionate pinch. "Smells like money, Little Kisses."

Mama refused to smile at this joke. She grimaced as if something tasted bitter in her mouth.

"That's our trunk!" Phoebe called as a beat-up black metal trunk with iron clamps flew through the air and landed with a thud on the platform.

Da hurried to retrieve their only piece of luggage. Dora saw him wince when he leaned over to pick up one end. He never liked to show that his back had been ruined by being thrown from a horse once too often. Stubbornly, he bit his moustache with his bottom teeth, hoisted the trunk on one broad shoulder, and staggered through the crowd again. "Come on," he barked and motioned with calloused, corded hands. The girls and their mother followed him through the depot.

"Well, I certainly hope nothing was broken," Mama said as if there were something valuable inside the trunk, something besides a couple of pairs of dancing shoes, half a dozen sequined costumes, and the good luck lasso Da took everywhere. He'd sold everything else that was valuable: his best saddle, his gun, his fancy roping shirts—even his pointed cowboy boots with the inlaid red leather stars. They were all gone, Dora knew. And everything else they owned—a few pieces of worn-out bedding, a chair, a few pots and pans, a cheap green cut-glass bowl—had been left where they'd sat. Wasn't time for a proper packing on this run, Da said. "Too many creditors," she'd heard him complain bitterly. Hadn't even been time to feed the cat before they rushed out the door. "Cat'll fend for itself," Da claimed.

Dora hoped he was right.

"This way," Da called. Dora and her sisters struggled to keep up with him as he shuffled along, winding and dodging between passengers.

Just when the girls thought the worst was over, they made their way out to the deafening street. Peddlers shouted. Crowds pushed and cursed and chattered. Whinnying horses thumped and clattered. Cable cars clanged. Reckless bicycle delivery boys hurled around horse-drawn carriages, hansoms, pushcarts, and pedestrians—all jostling for space. Moving at a snail's pace or stopped completely were every kind and shape of horse-drawn wagon—bakers' wagons with double pane glass, oil tankers, white ice wagons, pie carriers with side compartments, and furniture wagons with wide doors. Policemen in uniforms jounced along atop windowless Black Marias—wagons hauling prisoners to jail.

When Phoebe looked up she saw dark, looming buildings taller than anything she had ever seen before. She felt as if she were standing in the bottom of a canyon crisscrossed by electrical wires. The muted light hung heavily, a mixture of bitter coal smoke and choking dust. Flies buzzed. Along the edge of the sidewalk lay heaps of garbage—kitchen slops, cinders, broken cobblestones, horse manure, and dumped merchandise that smelled like bad eggs dissolved in ammonia.

Dora tried not to breathe through her nose as she toted her sister around overturned barrels and broken-down crates. A half-dozen laughing, ragged boys Lillian's age chased a growling dog. Mobs of grown-ups dodged gaslight poles and watering troughs and fire alarm boxes as they trudged along. With expressionless faces, Chicagoans stepped around beggars and the dead, bloated body of a horse on the sidewalk as if none of these were the least bit unusual.

"Wait for us!" Lillian shouted. She had caught the heel of her shoe in an open grate. With help from Phoebe, she managed to wrench her foot free.

Da turned. His face was bright red, and sweat streamed down his cheeks. His coat was stained with perspiration. "Hurry up!" he called and paused to study a street sign. "This way."

Obediently, Mama and the girls followed.

Every so often a cable car roared past, crammed with people sitting and standing. There was no horse. The clanging cable car seemed to move by magic. Lillian wondered if the cable car might be going where they were headed. She wanted to study the strange conveyance. She wanted to call to Da and see if they could ride such a marvel, but he was too far ahead for her to ask.

After what seemed forever, Da finally stopped a man and asked for directions. He lowered the trunk with a grunt and showed the man the tattered piece of paper. But the man with the dark beard couldn't read or speak English. He shook his head, shrugged his shoulders, and kept walking. Da asked another man. This skinny fellow gestured wildly and pointed. Phoebe felt spit fly out of his mouth onto her face. Worriedly, she wiped the spit away and hoped she would not be made crazy, too.

Finally, Da approached a policeman with a vast stomach and kindly eyes. He knew where Taylor Street was, and he used his billy club to point the way.

Dora and her sisters trudged on and on. Their stomachs growled with hunger. Dora wondered if they would ever eat again, if they would ever sleep again. Perhaps the rest of their lives were to be spent walking the sidewalks, dodging dogs and vendors and people and piles of garbage.

Finally, they found a four-story brick building with the address that matched the piece of paper. The building had steep front steps. Two boys perched on the railing carving their names with knives. They did not bother to look up when Dora and her family clambered past. The front door opened. Out stepped a heavyset woman with thinning gray hair. She brandished a broom and swatted at the boys, who fled for their lives. "Out!" she screamed. "And don't come back here."

"Ma'am, can you tell us where Mrs. Applebaum lives? We are here to rent rooms," Da said politely. He lowered the trunk to the top step.

"I'm her." She glanced quickly at the scribbled note. "Cody," she said in an unfriendly voice and snorted. "One of the Wild West folks, are you? Better not have no Indians with you. Don't take Indians in my tenement. And no dogs."

"No, ma'am. We have no Indians, no dogs," Da said wearily. "Can you show us the rooms?"

"Sure, sure," she replied. She motioned with one hand for them to follow her. "Cheap. Very cheap. Share the bathroom. Fourth floor." She huffed and puffed and pulled herself up the banister.

Mama sniffed and did not look impressed. The wallpaper in the dark hallway was stained and torn. The place smelled of cooked cabbage and fried onions, old smoke and burned porridge, unwashed clothes and ripening garbage. Dora and her sisters followed their parents up the stairs past rooms with the doors shut. They could hear snatches of voices through the paper-thin walls, the doors as thick as cardboard.

"Ain't got more than that. Should have asked him."

"Where's Binny?"

"Get out! And don't come back!"

When they finally reached the top floor, Mrs. Applebaum could not speak. She leaned heavily against a greasy wall to catch her breath. Then she reached into her apron pocket and produced a key. She jiggled the key in the lock and gave the door a hard kick.

The room was small and dank. The only window looked out on a brick wall. Two steel-spring beds with stained mattresses were shoved against one wall. Against another stood a table and two chairs. A calendar with a chromolith of a happy mother and child curled on the wall. Overhead ceiling plaster hung in shedding pieces.

"This the best you have?" Da demanded. He lowered the trunk, this time with such weariness Dora thought he'd never be able to lift the thing again.

Mrs. Applebaum nodded. "Rooms are hard to come by with the fair in town." She folded her arms across her ample chest. "Ordinarily, I don't rent to circus folks. Too undependable. I could get six dollars or more from regular tourists. Take it or leave it."

Someone screamed on the floor below them. Mrs. Applebaum stamped her foot on the floor. The screaming stopped.

"This small space is simply not acceptable," Mama said between gritted teeth to Da. "What is Colonel Cody thinking? We deserve better. Much better than this."

"What do you say?" Mrs. Applebaum said. She flicked a dead fly from the table with a rag tucked in her apron belt. "I got others wanting it. You don't rent, somebody else will."

Dora studied the airless room. This was worse than the tent in Reno, Nevada. Worse than living in the back of a dirty sheep herder's wagon in Tincup, Oregon. She tried not to look at her sisters' faces. She knew Phoebe and Lillian might burst into tears.

"Temporary," Da murmured to Mama. "Just for tonight. Just till I talk to Cody and get things settled."

Mama took a deep, angry breath. Her jaw twitched. But she didn't reply.

"We'll take it," Da said.

"Day's rent in advance," Mrs. Applebaum said and held out her hand. Da reached in his pocket and gave her two dollars in coins. She counted each coin before she handed over the key. "Bathroom's downstairs. Better keep your girls quiet. Don't like noisy brats." When she left, she slammed the door.

"Well," said Da cheerfully, "I think we can make the best of this."

Tess slid from Dora's arms to the floor. She waltzed away and peered under the bed. "Here kitty," she called. "Here kitty."

"Earl, you've got to go to Colonel Cody today," Mama insisted. "You've got to straighten this out. We can't stay here. This is horrible."

"Here kitty," Tess whispered.

"I'm hungry," Lillian said in a plaintive voice.

Phoebe bit her lip. "Where's the bathroom?"

"Girls, just a minute. Let me speak to your father," Mama said. She plunked her hatbox on the table and pulled off her gloves. "Earl, this cannot wait. You must see him today. Why is he treating us like this? We're star material. We deserve better."

Da shut his eyes tight and rubbed his temples with his fingers. "I'll see what I can do. Could sure use some sleep, though."

Mama pointed to the door. "We'll be waiting for you. Go talk to him. Now."

Da pushed his hat back on his head. "All right. All right."

Phoebe had slumped into the chair and was tracing circles in the dust on the table. Lillian sat perched on the very edge of the squeaky bed. "Mama, we're hungry. We're hungry. We're very hungry."

"Earl, we'll need some money," Mama called as he reached the door. "I have to feed them something."

Da sighed and handed her two dollar bills folded together tight. "I'll be back. Don't worry, Melba. Something will turn up. Everything will be fine."

"Don't forget to ask about the audition," Mama said, perking up as soon as she folded the money in her hand. Da nodded and shut the door behind him.

"Here kitty!" Tess called.

"What are you doing?" Mama demanded impatiently. "I wonder where I can get a new outfit for that audition. Don't you worry, girls. We'll be out of here in no time."

"Mama, we need something to eat. We got to have something to eat soon," Lillian cried. She held her stomach with both hands and leaned forward.

"All right. All right," Mama said. "I'll see what I can rustle up. Maybe a hand-held waffle or a sausage on a roll from one of the street vendors."

"Kitty!" Tess squealed. Something furry and small and gray rocketed past her feet and vanished in a hole in the wall.

"Rat!" Mama shrieked and jumped on the bed. Dora grabbed her youngest sister and hoisted her onto the table. Phoebe stood on a chair.

Only Lillian did not try to escape. She was laughing too hard. "Some kitty!" she said with tears rolling down her face.

Later that morning, after Mama had bought the girls some bread and a hunk of cheese and a wizened bunch of apples from a vendor on the street, Dora and her sisters felt sleepy. "You watch the others while I'm gone," Mama said, adjusting her hat.

"Where you going?" Dora asked nervously.

"To find something new to wear. I got fifty cents left. I mean to spend it on a pretty something nice for my audition. I'll be back. Don't let the girls roam. It's not safe."

This warning did not make Dora feel the least

bit encouraged. She watched the door shut quietly behind her mother and wondered what she would do when night came. What would she do when the rat came back? Luckily, her sisters had no energy to cause her trouble. Dora pried open the window as far as she could. She opened the trunk and found two sequined skirts, which she spread on the dirty mattress. Tess lay down and went right to sleep beside Lillian. Phoebe sat cross-legged on the other bed with her postcard and Lillian's pencil. She wrote in tiny letters in the margin:

Do you still beleeve in Happines-Ever-After?
In pure fresh contry air in Neb you cant
hardly imgagen wretchd Chicago streets

Discouraged, Phoebe sat and sat and couldn't think of anything more to write. Finally, she fell asleep. Dora placed the other chair against the door for their protection. She found a broken broomstick, which she held in her lap to keep watch for the next rat that darted out of the hole. No rat reappeared. It wasn't long before Dora nodded, arms folded, rested her forehead on the table, and slept.

When she awoke, she heard the sound of knocking. It was Mama. She bustled inside happy and overflowing with good news. She waved a new hat in Dora's face. It was red and beribboned with fake cherries. "Only cost me a nickel," she said breathlessly. She looked around the room at her sleeping daughters and frowned. "We got to get out of here. Look at this, Dora." She showed Dora a newspaper she had folded up inside her cape pocket.

Lillian awoke and made a mewling sound. Tess sat up and yawned. Dora wished her mother had not awakened them. Everything had been so peaceful. She had been dreaming she was back in Nebraska and it was the start of the new school year and she had a new Big Chief tablet of paper that smelled so wonderful and fresh that there were tears in her eyes. Mama danced around the room in the silly nickel hat. Dora spread the paper on the table and read aloud.

"Chicago's Fair is the foremost wonder of the World. The grounds of the Exposition, not far short of two square miles in area, are three times larger than the last World Fair in Paris. The grand Ferris Wheel rivals the Paris Eiffel Tower. The Manufactures building is the largest such structure on earth, covering twice the area of the Great Pyramid. The buildings are lit with 7,000 arc and 120,000 incandescent lamps, demonstrating the newfangled wonders of electricity ..."

Mama paused. "And just think, girls, we're going there! They call it the White City," she declared. "You are the luckiest children on earth."

Dora and her sisters were so excited that they forgot about feeling tired, dirty, hot, and hungry. "When can we go?" Lillian demanded.

"When can we see the fair?" Phoebe echoed.

Mama smiled mysteriously. "Soon. I'm sure of it. Chicago's a wonderful town."

Dora did not feel so certain. What little she had seen of Chicago had not impressed her very much. She began to wonder if Mama's description of the White City wasn't just more high-flown taradiddle. Dora knew that Mama embroidered reality to fit her fanciful, dramatic view of the way she wished things were. Mama was the only person Dora knew who could make a purse out of a sow's ear. Da lived on dreams, too. He colored them, flavored them to fit their circumstances. Dora had learned this long ago. As hard as she tried, she never felt enthralled. She never believed the next-best-thing, the fame-around-the-corner. Dreams did not feed her and nourish her the way they did Mama and Da.

An hour later, Da came home. He was grinning ear to ear. "Tomorrow," he said, "we go to Colonel Cody. All of us. You'll get to talk to him in person."

He winked at Mama, who seemed to flutter with happiness. "Tonight we go for dinner at a restaurant. What do you say to some big beefsteaks, my lovelies? Got my first paycheck already."

Dora and her sisters cheered. They had seldom eaten in restaurants. The idea was fantastic, incredible! They washed their faces in the leaky, yellow-stained bathroom faucet downstairs. Dora combed their hair. They piled down the steps, filled with delight and anticipation. Mama wore her new hat. She did not say one biting word to Da as they walked and walked and finally arrived at a fancy restaurant with menus and a man to wait on them with a white towel over one arm.

They ordered whatever they wished and did not have to share. The slabs of steaks filled their entire plates. The potatoes were as big as fists. Dora and her sisters ate until they felt as if they might explode. Their stomachs had never been so full, so satisfied. Tess happily nibbled on a steak bone. Neither Phoebe nor Lillian fought. Their parents smiled at each other. It was a wonderful evening. Dora tried desperately to memorize each second, terrified that she might wake up. It might only be a dream.

"You're awful quiet, Dora," Da said, wiping his moustache with a glorious big white napkin.

"Just thinking, that's all," Dora said. She smiled at her father. "What a day we've had."

"What a day is right!" Da leaned back and unwrapped a cigar. He bit off the tip, spit, and lit a wooden match using his thumb. "Just you wait. This is only the beginning. We're going to be rich. You bet. Colonel Cody's got an amazing operation. Biggest outfit I ever worked for in my life. You should see the crowds lined up to get in for the show."

"Rich," Mama murmured. She leaned forward with her chin in her hands, elbows on the table, and smiled dreamily. "Imagine all the hats and shoes and jewels I could buy if we were rich."

"I'd get a real house first thing," Phoebe said.

Lillian gave her sister a superior smirk. "I know something better. An elegant team and carriage. That way everybody will see me and feel jealous."

Everyone laughed. "What about you, Dora?" Phoebe asked.

Dora smiled shyly. "School," she said. "I'd go to school."

Lillian snorted. "That's a waste of good money if you ask me. What do you think, Little Kisses?"

Tess didn't even bother to look up. She was too busy gnawing steak bones and licking butter from her fingers.

Da finished his cigar. "Time to go. We have a busy day ahead of us, my lovelies."

Instinctively, Dora tucked the last of the dinner rolls into her pockets. Mama stood and ushered the three other girls past the other diners toward the restaurant door. It was a crowded, smoky place. Dora waited for her father. She watched him as he counted out the money from his pocket to pay the bill, fishing deep in his coat for the last necessary coins. When he looked up and saw her watching him, something like irritation flitted across his face.

Dora looked away and drew in a sharp breath. She knew. Da had not said one word, and yet she was certain. He had just spent every last cent he had on their fine, fancy dinner.

All the way home from the restaurant while her sisters were singing, "Ta-ra-ra-boom-de-yah" and their parents were walking arm-in-arm, Dora worried where they would sleep tomorrow and how they'd pay for their next meal.

Chapter

3

The next day the wind shifted. The stench from the stockyards blew away from the city and out into the lake. The sky shone bright blue. Da, Mama, Dora, and her sisters packed their few belongings in the trunk, left the tenement, and arrived at the Wild West Show grounds by mid-morning. Crowds milled about. Lillian could hardly breathe, she felt so excited. From a distance she could make out the roofs and snapping flags of the tall white buildings of the World's Columbian Exposition behind the gate across the street. Colonel Cody's grandstand for 18,000 spectators and his 15 leased acres were located on an empty, flat piece of land outside the entrance to the World's Columbian Exposition.

"Will we see him?" Lillian asked Da eagerly as they walked past the ticket booths with great banners flapping in the breeze.

Da smiled. "Sure. Sure." He shifted the trunk on his shoulder.

"Do you think he might give me his autograph?" Lillian said. Everyone knew about glamorous, heroic Buffalo Bill—Pony Express rider, Indian tracker, and intrepid hunter, who gunned down 4,280 buffalo in just eighteen months. His brave stage coach rescues were celebrated in countless penny novels. Newspapers reported how he and his Wild West Show had performed amazing stunts before kings and queens in Europe.

"I hear he is very handsome," Mama said.

"Tolerable so," Da replied. "You'll see for yourself."

The girls followed their father through a camp of tents inhabited by terrifying-looking Indians and ponies decorated with feathers and paint. Dora held Tess very tight as they hurried past a group of men crouched on the ground in fringed pants and feathers in their braided hair. One man saw Phoebe staring at him. He took a knife from his belt and brandished it in a menacing manner. Phoebe flinched.

The Indian's companion made a polite bow. "Miss, do not pay any attention to this rogue," he said in a precise English accent.

The other Indian smiled a toothy smile.

Da lifted his free hand to his hat brim to signal a greeting. "You from Dakota?"

The Indians shook their heads. "London," the grinning one replied.

When they reached Buffalo Bill's official tent, Phoebe held Dora's hand very tightly. Da knocked on the broad tent post, then set the trunk down. "Yes, who is it?" came a mellow voice from inside.

"Earl Pomeroy, sir. The new horse handler. You said for me to come today to see you."

One of Buffalo Bill's attendants, who wore a cowboy hat and had a large wad of chewing tobacco tucked in one cheek, opened the tent flap. Lillian couldn't help herself. She peeked inside.

"Five minutes. That's all you get," the attendant mumbled through his wad of tobacco, and then stepped outside. "I'll watch your gear."

"Come in! Come in!" Buffalo Bill bellowed. He sat very straight in a chair covered with black-and-white rawhide. There was something regal in his appearance. It was as if he was holding court in his dark cutaway coat. His shirt was trimmed with a long collar, and around his neck was a large four-hand tie. Phoebe stared at the stick pin in his tie with three mysterious feathers. She was too embarrassed to look directly into his curious brown eyes. He wore his curling brown hair combed back nearly to his shoulders. His neat moustache and beard on his chin were only beginning to turn gray.

The tent was decorated with stuffed animal heads and various posters and gifts from his travels. It was almost as if the place were a kind of display and 47-year-old Buffalo Bill was one of the many famous decorations. "Well, well, who have we here?" Buffalo Bill said. He smiled at the four girls. Clearly, he enjoyed the presence of young admirers.

"Hello," Lillian said in a small voice and made a quick curtsy. She had imagined Buffalo Bill differently. Where was his snowy white horse? His light buckskin shirt, his crimson shirt, his broad sombrero or the Springfield rifle he'd named Lucretia Borgia? She had hoped for a bold hunter, and hostile Indian killer, a gallant sportsman—not a mild-mannered, middle-aged man. "How do you do? My name is Lillian Lucille Marie Pomeroy, and I would like to be in your show."

Da coughed nervously. Even Mama, who was

ordinarily very talkative, was too shocked by Lillian's bold comment to speak.

The corners of Buffalo Bill's eyes crinkled with wrinkles as if he was going to laugh, but he thought better of the idea and let his eyes smile instead. "I see," he said. "And what about your sisters? What are your names?"

"Dora," Dora said hoarsely.

Phoebe stared at her feet and whispered her name.

"Tess!" Tess said and pulled her dress up over her head in a very unbecoming fashion. Right on cue, she began to chant a poem she had learned from her sisters:

> *"Buffalo Bill, Buffalo Bill,*
> *Never missed and never will,*
> *Always aims and shoots to kill,*
> *And the company pays his buffalo bill."*

Buffalo Bill burst into laughter. Dora didn't think her sister's performance was the least bit entertaining. Quickly, red-faced Dora adjusted her sister's clothing. She felt absolutely mortified. Why had they ever taught her that rhyme? She concentrated her gaze on the beautiful, expensive saddle inlaid with silver and precious gems.

"Maybe you got some real talent here, Pomeroy." Buffalo Bill turned to the girls. "Do you ride?"

Dora bit her lips tight. Phoebe shook her head. "I do," Lillian boasted. "I can shoot, too."

"Then you might enjoy watching Annie Oakley. She was just about your age when she began doing trick shooting and riding. Why, Little Missie's the best there is. Sitting Bull named her Little Sure Shot. I've seen her blast a ten-cent piece held between an attendant's thumb and forefinger at a distance of thirty feet."

Lillian gulped. She knew she couldn't beat that.

"You are most kind to let my daughters visit you," Mama said. She fluttered her eyelashes. Da gave her a warning look that she pretended not to see. "Now I know you've hired my husband, Earl, to be your horse handler, and what I'm wondering is if you'd consider allowing me to audition. I have several popular songs memorized. I can ride like the wind. And I can supply my own glamorous outfits."

Buffalo Bill burst into laughter. Mama turned bright red. Dora frowned to see her mother so humiliated.

"Well, ma'am, with the exception of Annie Oakley, my one trick shooter, I haven't any parts for white women in my acts. And we don't have a chorus line in the Wild West Show," he said, chuckling. "In fact, I don't like to have any women anywhere on the premises after hours of the show. I don't let the men bring their wives—and certainly not their pretty daughters—to live in camp. Causes too many problems. Didn't you read your contract, Mr. Pomeroy?"

Da's expression collapsed. Now it was his turn to look embarrassed. He gave Mama a quick, desperate sidewise glance as if she'd just caught him playing poker. "Where . . . where are they going to live, sir?" he asked slowly. "The tenement you suggested for the first night—"

"Let me explain, Mr. Pomeroy," Buffalo Bill interrupted. He ran his fingers quickly through his hair. "Your contract says your job is to live near the horses. You train them. You oversee grooming. You protect them from local horse thieves."

Da blinked hard. "Horse thieves?"

"Unlike the fair, we don't have seventeen hundred Columbian guards or two hundred and fifty undercover Pinkerton plainclothes detectives to watch our goods," Buffalo Bill said. He motioned to his servant as if to indicate that their interview was over.

"But, sir," Da persisted, "where is my family

going to live? The tenement is really too . . . too awful." He paused when he saw his wife giving him an encouraging look. "And too expensive."

"That is not my problem. You should have left your family in Nebraska." Buffalo Bill rose from his chair. He was not nearly as tall as Dora thought he would be. In fact, he was rather slight. "You can take the job according to the contract you signed, or you can be replaced. It's that simple. There are one hundred fifty men just like you waiting for this job."

Da bit his lip and signaled for his family to follow him out the door. Lillian grabbed him by the sleeve to stop him. She had no intention of going back to Nebraska. "The White City," she hissed. "What about the White City?"

Da turned, took a deep breath, and tried one more time. "What if my wife and girls can find a place to live and work across the street at the fair? I can live here, just the way the contract says. Surely, sir, you must have connections over there—"

Buffalo Bill held up one hand to stop Da from going any further. He pulled out his gold pocket watch, flipped it open, and checked the time. "The Wild West Show has been shunned by the Lady Managers and the formidable Queen Bertha

Palmer. She thinks she runs everything. According to her, we're just not highbrow enough."

"But, sir," Da pleaded. "My wife and daughters will do anything, live anywhere." He twisted the end of his moustache nervously with his fingers. "The truth of the matter is that I haven't got any money to send them all the way back to Nebraska—or even to my wife's folks in Salt Creek Valley, Kansas, for that matter."

Mama flashed a charming, stagy smile at Buffalo Bill. "Certainly a big, handsome, intelligent man like you must have other connections in the White City. Don't you know anyone who could—"

"Did you say Salt Creek Valley?" Buffalo Bill asked. He stood motionless with his watch open. The ticking noise seemed to grow louder and louder. No one spoke.

"That's right, sir," Da said and cleared his throat. "My wife's family's lived there ever so long."

Buffalo Bill clicked the watch shut and tucked it inside his pocket. He stared into space for several moments, as if he were studying in his mind how to spell aloud a very difficult word like *hyperbole*. Dora watched him, fascinated.

"My folks have lived in Kansas since the 1850s,

I guess," Mama said. She spoke slowly, carefully. "Maiden name's Farley."

"Farley. Farley." Buffalo Bill sat down in his chair again. "I recollect the Farley farm. Not far from where my father had his homestead. Pa died in 1857. Some pro-slavery fool stabbed him in the chest." He shook his head. "I was just eleven. Almost your age," he said and looked at Dora.

Dora squirmed. "Sorry you lost your father." She pushed her toe into the plush carpet that covered the wooden tent platform. She wondered if Buffalo Bill really slept in this tent. Did he have nightmares about his pa?

"Cody?" a voice called from outside. "We got some important folks out here waiting to see you."

"In a minute, Fred," Buffalo Bill called back. He looked up at Da and Mama as if he'd forgotten they were there. From his shiny wooden desk he took out a piece of paper and scribbled something. From one of the many drawers he produced purple ticket-sized pieces of paper. He turned to Da and handed him these. "Nothing works like a box seat to convince anyone of anything," he said. "There's a new dormitory for women just finished on the lakefront. Built by the Lady Managers, as they like to call themselves. Listen closely. On this paper is the name and the address inside the fair of one of my admirers, who runs the dormitory. You tell her I sent you. She'll give your wife and girls a room." He shook his head as if with a sense of disbelief. "Farley. Don't that beat all?"

Mama smiled, determined to press her luck even further. "You have been so kind. Do you think, sir, that you might have somewhere in one of those fancy desk drawers complimentary fair passes for me and my girls? Costs fifty cents for me and twenty-five cents admission for them each time we go in. Going to be pretty difficult working if we can't afford to get inside every day."

Da sucked in his breath as if his wife had really gone and done it this time. He always said Mama was so stubborn and ornery to get her way that if she drowned, they'd have to look for her body upstream.

Miraculously, Buffalo Bill did not refuse Mama's request. "Spunk," he said, chuckling. "That's what you need in this business." He pulled open another drawer and produced five green complimentary fair passes and signed each one.

"An autograph!" Lillian whispered. "Oh, thank you. Thank you, sir."

The other girls thanked him as well. Quickly, Da ushered the group out of the tent. "Sir, you don't know what this means to us. A new start."

"Don't mention it," Buffalo Bill said in a gruff voice, then added, "now get to work before I change my mind."

Da picked up the trunk. Armed now with the precious passes and the name on the piece of paper, Da, Mama, and the girls crossed Stony Island Avenue and walked south toward the official fair exit on 64th Street. "Once I get my gear stowed, I'll send this trunk over to the dormitory today," Da told Mama.

"Good-bye, Da," Tess called. "Don't forget Nancy in the trunk." Lillian was so busy craning her neck for sight of the Ferris wheel that she barely waved to their father. Only Dora, Tess, and Phoebe watched their parents exchange dramatic farewells—mostly for the benefit of the growing crowd of visitors waiting outside the ticket gate.

"Good-bye, my darling," Mama called and waved a handkerchief.

Da swept off his hat and threw a noisy kiss.

Dora blushed. She felt embarrassed by her parents' display. At the same time, she knew she'd miss her father. "Let's go to the White City," she said and herded her sisters toward the gate. They had to wait with their mother nearly half an hour before it was their turn to enter.

"Here are our passes," Mama said in a regal

voice. Then she flashed a piece of paper that said, Miss Sada Harrington, Women's Building. "We are trying to find this individual. Can you help us?" Then she added, as if she couldn't help herself, "We are close friends of Bertha's."

"Bertha?"

Mama sniffed. "Mrs. Bertha Palmer."

The ticket taker was so impressed that he allowed Mama and the girls to cut ahead of a dozen people. "Right this way, madame."

The girls eagerly scrambled through the gate. The fair at last! "Who is Bertha Palmer?" Dora asked Mama when they were out of earshot of the ticket taker.

Mama shrugged. "Royalty, I guess."

Chapter

4

The bigness of the fair overwhelmed and bewildered Dora and her sisters. "Stupendous!" Dora muttered, using her favorite spelling word. She glanced at towering, fluted columns so wide that it would take two grown-ups with arms outstretched to reach around one.

"Like a dream," Lillian said. She squinted at the blinding, pure white buildings. Colorful flags snapped and flapped in the wind atop the towering roofs.

Phoebe, who measured all beauty on the basis of Wards Catalog, was too speechless to speak.

"Boats!" Tess screamed and jumped up and down. Sleek gondolas and electrically driven crafts with striped awnings glided over vast ponds and canals. Bridges spanned the sparkling water. Marble steps led down to a peaceful, lapping basin that reflected the stark white buildings. Bright flowers overflowed from enormous, oversized urns. Dora and her sisters stood transfixed. It was as if they had entered a whole new land, an exotic country from a fairy tale.

Everywhere well-dressed people roamed in pairs, in groups, alone. Men wore derbies or top hats. Women had fancy hats and carried parasols. Every so often the visitors stopped and gawked and pointed. Some took photographs with little black box cameras. Others walked quickly, scarcely taking time to observe where they were going. None of the fair visitors looked ragged. No one looked hungry. The well-fed faces seemed filled with a kind of happy anticipation, as if something wonderful would happen to them any moment.

Phoebe spied no heaps of garbage or manure. She heard no sound of wagon wheels grinding or horses whinnying and clip-clopping along. Everything seemed orderly, almost eerily quiet. Lillian sniffed the air. The scent of chocolate and ripe bananas and fresh popcorn and lavender hair oil filled her nose—none of the smells she remembered from the streets of Chicago. "Heaven looks like this," Lillian murmured. "Where's the Ferris wheel?"

"What if we get separated?" Phoebe asked. She bit her nails and scanned the infinitely wide plaza. And what lay beyond that? More buildings, more plazas, more avenues, more crowds. "We'll never find each other again." Suddenly she felt as if she might throw up.

Tess stared at the ground in fascination. "Penny!" she said triumphantly and picked up a glittering coin. She studied another patch of ground and discovered a lost ladies' glove smashed and flattened into the pavement. It looked like a hand pointing in some mysterious direction. Determinedly, Tess tried to pry the twisted fingers apart. "Look, Dorie!" she said and pulled on Dora's skirt.

"Yes, yes," Dora said absentmindedly. She was too busy admiring the spectacular sweep of glass windows in the next building. "Don't play with that dirty thing, Tess."

Tess pouted and dropped the glove. There was nothing the least bit interesting to her about architecture. She could care less about the inspiring statues or the grand murals.

"So many fancy people," Mama said. Self-consciously, she tucked a wisp of hair inside her fake-cherry hat, which suddenly seemed very shabby indeed. She glanced at the paper in her hand. "Women's Building. Where's that? I suppose I'd better ask someone." She hurried across the plaza to a man in a uniform standing beside a fruit stand.

As her mother walked away from them, Dora felt very small—the same sense she'd had the first time she'd walked out into the enormous openness of the Nebraska plains. The fair's bigness made Dora feel insignificant. She wished Da were there. He always had a way of making everything seem all right.

When their mother returned she pointed north. "We have to walk that way. Past the Transportation Building and the Choral Hall and something called the Horticulture Building." She looked confused.

"Where's the Ferris wheel?" Lillian demanded.

"We're not going to the Ferris wheel," Dora said impatiently. She took Tess's hand. "We've got to find a place to live."

"Do you suppose there are houses here?" Phoebe asked hopefully as they began to walk along. The Transportation Building, which faced a great pool of water, seemed to go on and on forever. Unlike the other buildings, it was dark colored. Maybe they could live there.

Tess raced ahead, jumping from one concrete square to the next near the railing. She scarcely noticed the great glittering arch over the Transportation Building doorway. She was too busy hurling pebbles into the water and shouting at the ducks.

"You suppose that's real gold?" Lillian said, pointing at the arches.

"Don't even think about it," Phoebe warned.

"I'm not stealing nothing," Lillian said and marched ahead.

Out on the lagoon was a strange two-masted boat and a few small islands with scrubby trees and bushes. Phoebe paused and looked out at the islands. "We could live out there in a tent," she suggested to Dora. "We'd have to use the boat. Maybe nobody'd mind."

Dora rolled her eyes. "We don't have a tent. Come on," she said and tugged her sister's arm.

"Girls!" Mama called.

Dora and her sisters raced to catch up. They raced and wove their way among the enormous fat white columns of Choral Hall and played leapfrog in front of the Horticulture Building with the great glass dome that reminded Phoebe of Mama's beautiful glass bowl turned upside down. It was too bad they'd had to sell that bowl.

"Feet hurt!" Tess cried. Her face was red, and she was staggering dramatically beneath the fighting statues. When she noticed what a satisfying echo her voice made, she shouted louder. "Feet hurt! Feet hurt!"

A man in a uniform limped out of the Horticulture entrance and scowled at Tess. Maybe his feet hurt, too, Dora thought.

"Pick her up, Dora," Mama said wearily.

Dora did as she was told. As she walked past another unfriendly man in the open Horticulture door, she felt a warm, humid breeze that smelled heavy with the fragrance of flowering plants and dirt. A sign said, CRYSTAL CAVE FIFTY CENTS.

"What do you suppose is Crystal Cave?" Phoebe asked Lillian.

Lillian shrugged. "I'm thirsty." She stared at the little kiosk with the pointed roof. "Wish we had some money to buy one of those soda waters that make your nose fizz."

"Well, we don't, so keep walking," Dora murmured. Everything at the fair was going to cost money—the one thing her family had in very short supply.

On and on they marched until at last, after what seemed like forever, they reached the Women's Building, with the winged angels on the roof and great potted urns filled with purple blossoms. "Here we are," Mama said.

Wearily, the girls climbed up the steps past picnickers eating bologna and crackers and cold chicken. Dora licked her lips. She had to grab Tess before she scooped up a discarded, fresh pastry rind smeared with strawberry jam.

"Ducks!" Tess shouted and pointed. The fat white birds waddled around the benches and railings and hungrily nibbled crumbs and breadcrusts. A sign posted in the doorway announced, CORN DODGER COOKING DEMONSTRATION AT 2 P.M.

"Do you suppose they give free samples?" Lillian said eagerly.

Inside the door, Mama and the girls found themselves in a great, cool room with a massive, seventy-five-foot-tall ceiling. The walls were filled with pottery and stained glass and fabric. The girls had to lean their heads back very far to see the great paintings high up on the walls and statues of valiant women everywhere.

"Hello!" Tess shouted just to hear her echo.

"Shut up, Tess," Dora warned. She followed their mother to a desk, where a severe-looking woman with a faint moustache looked at her piece of paper, then handed it to someone else who looked at it and then handed it to someone else.

"Take the elevator," the woman with the moustache finally said. "To the second floor. The rooms are arranged along a corridor opening through arches over the great Rotunda. Next to the Assembly Hall, you'll see the Model Corn Kitchen. There's a door there, just to the left. That's Miss Harrington's office. Do you understand?"

Mama nodded even though she looked very confused. "This way to the elevator. I saw a sign," Lillian said and pointed. Nervously, Mama and the girls entered the doorway. They had never been in an elevator before. The small, dark space reminded Dora of a chicken coop.

"I want to get out—" Phoebe said. Too late. The door slid shut with a menacing whisper. Nothing happened. Tess whimpered.

"Now what?" Mama said desperately.

On the wall was a row of buttons. Dora pressed all of them. The elevator jerked and rumbled dangerously. Phoebe screamed. "We'll all be killed!" Lillian whispered.

Suddenly, the elevator door opened. Dora and her sisters did not need to be urged to scamper out as quickly as possible. Everything looked strange. "Where are we?" Mama asked.

"This way," Lillian replied, pointing.

By the time they located Miss Harrington's office, Dora felt as if she might collapse. Mama straightened her hat and told the girls to wait quietly outside. "You're in charge, Dora," Mama said. "Don't let the girls wander off." She knocked on the door briskly. The door opened. Mama disappeared inside.

Minutes passed. Tess practiced sliding down the smooth, cool hallway floor. Phoebe and Lillian explored the endless corridor. When they returned, both Tess and Dora were delighted to discover that their sisters carried handfuls of baked samples from the Corn Kitchen. The sweet corn dodgers were as big as fist-sized griddle cakes. Dora quickly divided up their spoils so that everyone had equal shares.

"More!" Tess cried and clapped her hands together.

"How'd you get these?" Dora asked, licking her fingers.

"Put two cups of white corn meal in a bowl," Phoebe said with great enthusiasm as she stuffed another chunk of corn dodger in her mouth. "Pour over it sufficient boiling water to scald, being exceedingly careful to just moisten the meal and stir all the time—"

"What a show-off in front of those ladies with the puffy hats!" Lillian interrupted. "You should have seen Phoebe, Dora. Acting like she knew all about shortening and baking pans. She lied and said our family always ate a good, nutritious breakfast together every morning. We don't even have a stove no more!"

"Any more," Dora said and sighed. What were they going to do if Mama failed to convince Miss Harrington? Where would they sleep that night?

Suddenly, the door opened. Mama walked outside beaming. "And thank you so much, ma'am!"

"Yes, of course," another voice said from inside. "I am so happy to help another one of our own in need. It gives me pleasure. God bless you!"

The door shut. Mama smiled at the girls.

"You got a place, didn't you?" Dora said happily.

"Yes, indeed I did, thanks to Colonel William F. Cody. The Women's Dormitory on Ellis Avenue. We'll take the cable car."

The girls hurried out into the sunlight again. While Phoebe and Lillian seemed more excited about taking a cable car ride, Dora was simply happy to have a roof over their heads.

Mama spent her last twenty-five cents for their five fares. She and the girls climbed into the horseless cable car, a small open vehicle with seats on both sides. Some riders held on to loops hanging from the ceiling. The grip-man stood in front and threw a great lever. The cable car lurched up the street. The car hummed loudly and followed a deep slot in the street that made a menacing sound. Underground a long cable moved and pulled the cable car along.

"It'll cost us a nickel each to get back and forth to the fair," Dora shouted at Mama over the noise of the cable car.

"That's right," Mama said, as if this news was just another unpleasant detail. "You worry too much, Dora."

Dora frowned. "But we have no more money. How will we pay for our housing? How will we eat tonight?"

"Something will turn up," Mama said in her gayest, theatrical voice. "Something always turns up."

Dora did not feel the least bit confident. All they'd had to eat that day were the stale rolls she'd saved from the restaurant and the corn dodger samples. Her stomach was beginning to roar with hunger.

The Women's Dormitory was a simple two-story frame structure on the lakefront about one mile from the north end of the fairgrounds. Mama marched up to the front door and knocked loudly. A woman named Miss Starkweather answered.

She was a short, wide woman who wore a great sash that said Welcome in pink letters. Mama explained who they were and why they had come and who had sent them. "We have special permission from Miss Harrington," Mama said and showed her the scribbled note from Buffalo Bill.

"I'm afraid we're full," Miss Starkweather replied. Her smile was not nearly as friendly-looking as her sash.

Mama looked stunned. "That's impossible. Miss Harrington said—"

"So sorry." Miss Starkweather began to shut the door on them.

Dora felt awful. What a disaster! Now where would they sleep? Where would they eat? Lillian and Phoebe began to sniffle.

"I think you should look again to see if something's available," Mama said in her most stubborn voice. From her pocketbook she slipped out the purple complimentary passes that said Wild West Show in big letters. She used the passes like a fan in front of her smiling face. Then she tapped Miss Starkweather on the pudgy arm. "Go look again, will you, ma'am?"

Miss Starkweather cleared her throat. She went inside. She came back. Her face was flushed.

"Well, what a surprise. We do have a room that just opened up."

"Excellent," Mama said. Without saying one word, she neatly stacked the Wild West Show passes and presented them to Miss Starkweather.

Miss Starkweather looked quickly over her shoulder, then stuffed the passes into her pocket behind the Welcome sash. "Luggage?" she demanded in a businesslike fashion.

"No," said Mama, her voice bright and cheerful. "My husband will be sending it along."

Miss Starkweather gave them a quick tour. "Facility sleeps one thousand. It's completely constructed of Georgia pine."

"Smells like a Christmas tree," Phoebe said, sniffing.

"The building is only one month old," Miss Starkweather continued, clearly not happy to be interrupted by a child. "This way. Each freshly painted room has a window overlooking the street, the backyard, or the inner court. There are eight bright and sunny parlors. Four of the rooms have coal-burning fireplaces. We don't expect to use these much, since the building will only be open until late October."

"Late October?" Mama asked and frowned.

"When the fair ends," Miss Starkweather said. "Come along."

"What's the matter, Mama?" Dora whispered.

"Nothing," Mama said and laughed gaily. "Isn't this the prettiest place?"

Excitedly, the girls poked their heads into one of the parlors, which was inhabited by a group of unhappy-looking older women in black. Most of them were reading or sewing. The group of sight-seeing nurses, pious spinsters, and vacationing schoolteachers did not seem pleased to see Dora and her sisters.

"Hello!" Tess said and waved a sticky hand.

One woman waved back.

"Come now, step lively," Miss Starkweather said. "As you may know, most fairgoers have to pay high prices in the downtown for hotels—as much as six dollars a day. Thanks to the farsighted Mrs. Bertha Palmer, you and many others are bene-fitting from the Women's Dormitory Association investment. You only have to pay fifty cents a day for yourself and twenty-five cents a day for each child."

"A wonderful bargain," Mama said appreciatively.

Their tour guide opened the door to their clean, sunny room. The girls were stunned. "Even the furniture matches!" Phoebe said. "Just like Wards Catalog!"

There was a double bed and a single bed with

just enough room for one extra wire-spring cot. Lillian waltzed around and around. "And look at the dressing table with a looking glass!" she said happily.

A washstand and a chair made up the rest of the furnishings. "Each room is lit by candles, but the halls and sitting rooms have gas light," Miss Starkweather said. "I hope your daughters are aware of fire hazards?"

Mama nodded. "Oh yes. They've grown up around stage lights all their life."

Miss Starkweather shot a critical glance at Mama. "You're in the theater business? Not a very proper occupation for a woman with children, I should say. We don't usually rent to actresses."

"Oh," said Mama quickly, "I'm not an actress right now."

Miss Starkweather put her fists on her hips and frowned. "I should hope not. Now if everything is in order, I'd like to explain to you our rules. No men allowed. No cooking in the rooms. No liquor and no smoking. No loud noises. Our guests are refined ladies. They don't like to be disturbed." She stared hard at Dora and her boisterous sisters. "How long do you plan on staying here?"

"As long as we can," Mama said, trying hard to smile.

Miss Starkweather made a loud *humph.* "Twenty-five days will cost thirty-seven dollars and fifty cents for you and all your daughters."

Mama gulped. "Thirty-seven dollars and fifty cents?" The woman might as well have said thirty-seven million dollars.

"And when the twenty-five days are up, we'll review your behavior and see if we can extend your stay any further. It's not our policy, however, I should warn you. Many people have been waiting to stay here. You've been given lodging only because of Colonel Cody."

Mama tried to appear meek and grateful. "I know. A wonderful man." She looked around at the room, which was more beautiful than anything they had ever lived in in their whole lives.

"Good home-cooked meals are available in a redbrick house next door for dormitory residents only. Breakfast costs twenty-five cents. Dinner with three courses costs fifty cents. If you don't have any more questions, I'll be leaving. And please remember, the Travelers' Aid Society is always here to help you."

As she disappeared down the hall, a door opened nearby. A thin woman in a dark dress came closer. She was smiling at Mama, who suddenly seemed very tired and pale. "Hello," she said, smiling at Mama and Dora and the girls. "I guess we'll be neighbors. My name is Julia Shattuck."

Mama nodded and introduced herself.

"I work over at the Children's Building as a nursemaid. I'm from South Dakota. Where are you from?" Julia asked.

"Everywhere, I guess." Mama struggled to smile. "You know of any jobs over there? I've got to find a way to pay the rent for myself and my daughters."

"I can personally recommend the Roof Garden Cafe."

"They need entertainers?"

Julia laughed. "No, I heard today that they're looking for a new waitress. The restaurant's at the top floor of the Women's Building. Best apple pie at the fair. Jobs are tight. I'd recommend you go right away before someone else snatches it."

"Thanks for the information," Mama said and herded the girls into the room. She took off her hat only long enough to comb her hair and put her hat back on again.

"Where are you going, Mama?" Phoebe demanded.

"To get that job, if it's still available," Mama said. She kissed each of her daughters. "Dora, watch everyone. I'll be back as soon as I can. I'm going to have to walk back to the fair." She left before Dora could ask her what she was supposed to feed her hungry sisters.

"She better come back," Phoebe said in a worried voice.

"Hungry!" Tess whined.

Phoebe nodded. "We'll starve."

The girls stretched out on the luxurious beds. All except Lillian, who stood in front of the mirror and practiced a little dance step. "No one's going to starve," Lillian said sweetly to her reflection in the mirror. She made a little twirl, turned the doorknob, and opened the door.

"Where are you going?" Dora demanded. "You heard Mama. Nobody's supposed to leave my sight."

"I'll be right back. I'm going to buy us some dinner in the redbrick building across the way."

"Dinner?" Phoebe demanded. "How?"

Lillian slipped off her worn shoe and produced two dimes and a nickel from the inside of her sock. "It's amazing what you can find on the fairgrounds if you keep a sharp eye."

Before Dora could protest, Lillian scampered away to the restaurant next door. She came back with a plate heaping with sweet potatoes, chicken,

corn, and a stack of five pieces of white bread. The
girls sat around the plate, which was placed in the
middle of the floor. Each sister passed the fork and
took an equal-sized bite in turn. Somehow, by eating very slowly, the one dinner seemed to fill all
four of them up.

Chapter

5

The next day Dora awoke and forgot where she was. Sun streamed through the window of their room in the Women's Dormitory, and for a moment she thought she was back on the ranch. She sat up and stretched. Then she remembered. They were in Chicago. She counted her sisters: one, two, three. And the lump that was their mother. "Only Da's missing," she thought sadly. She wondered how he was doing at the Wild West Show and Congress of Rough Riders.

She crept from her bed quietly in order to awaken snoring Phoebe. At the window Dora already heard the sounds of the city—a cacophony of hammering and horses and the steady bass rumble of the cable car machinery under the street.

Chicago could not compare with the White City. The fair, she decided, was a kind of magical kingdom where nothing terrible could ever happen.

Hanging on the back of the chair she saw an apron and a plain blue dress with a severe collar. That could only mean one thing. Mama had the job! Dora shook Lillian's shoulder to tell her the good news. But somehow Lillian wasn't interested. "Leave me alone. I'm dreaming about my show," she said in a sleepy voice.

Slowly, carefully, Dora crept out of the room and down the hall to the bathroom that all the rooms shared. She could hear voices coming from downstairs, and she crept to the landing. Out the front door she saw a line of women in hats carrying luggage—a line that stretched nearly three blocks.

"This is no shanty," one of the dormitory employees told an enormous woman with a large hat with a turquoise feather.

"I am a New Hampshire stockholder. I specifically requested that someone meet me at the train. No one came. And now you tell me I must sleep in the parlor," the woman said indignantly. "That is simply not acceptable."

"I am sorry, but there are no more regular accommodations."

Dora crept away anxiously back to their room. Soon they would need to pay the rent. Wasn't that what Miss Starkweather had said? If they didn't pay on time, there were plenty of paying customers who'd like to have their room. Dora shut the door. She inspected Mama's apron. Suddenly, she had another awful thought. "Mama?" she said, shaking her mother's shoulder.

"What?"

"When you supposed to be at work?"

"Breakfast shift."

"Breakfast!" Dora gasped. "You better get up. You've overslept."

Like a shot, Mama leapt from the bed and quickly dressed in her uniform. She hastily threw water on her face and struggled to comb her hair. "My hat!" she screamed. Dora handed her the hat and her pocketbook.

"Good luck!" Phoebe sang out.

Mama growled something no one could hear. The door slammed. Dora prayed that she'd get there on time. Mama was not a morning person. It had always been Dora's job to start the cookstove fire and make breakfast for everyone on the ranch.

"She doesn't look too happy anymore," Phoebe said, remembering the happy, hopeful Mama from the train.

"At least she's got a job," Phoebe reminded her. She began making the bed.

"She'd rather be performing," Lillian said.

Dora and Phoebe knew she was right. Mama wasn't happy when she wasn't on stage. But they needed this job, and they needed this money. Somehow Dora was going to have to make sure Mama got to work on time—if she hadn't lost the job already.

"Ta-ra-ra-boom-dee-yah! Ta-ra-ra-boom-dee-yah!" Tess chanted and jumped from bed to bed. Soon Lillian and Phoebe joined her, and the whole room of Georgia pine walls and ceiling began to shake ominously.

It wasn't long before there was a loud knocking on the door. "This is a house of quiet!" someone shouted. "I'll remind you to follow our rules or be removed."

Dora grabbed Tess in midair. She made a threatening sign to Lillian and Phoebe to stop jumping at once. "Yes, ma'am," she said sweetly. "Get dressed," she said under her breath to her sisters. "Now!"

"You're bossy," Lillian said and pouted. "Who said you're in charge?"

"Mama," Dora replied in a threatening voice. "While she's gone, I'm in charge."

"We still have Da," Phoebe said in a rebellious voice.

"But we don't know when he's going to come back. In the meantime, you better obey me—or else." Dora made a fist.

Her sisters weren't impressed. Lillian sat on the bed and scowled. "You're no fun."

Dora could sense that she was quickly losing control of her sisters. She was going to have to get all three of them out of the building before they were permanently thrown out. The only way she knew how to do that was to distract them. "Who wants to go to the fair?" Dora said in a quiet, sly voice.

"We do!" the girls sang out.

"Quiet!" the angry voice shot back.

Dora put her fingers to her lips. "Then let's go. Clean up. Make your beds. Comb your hair. Wash your faces. Don't forget the fair passes. Mama left them on top of the dressing table. Last one done is a rotten egg."

The girls quickly finished their chores. Dora handed them each half a piece of dry bread saved from their dinner the night before. They gnawed hungrily and walked in silence single-file down the hallway. Gray heads stuck out of several bedroom doors. Their neighbors made disapproving noises at the girls, who dribbled crumbs on the clean pine floor. The women from the Travelers' Aid Society sitting at the main desk looked at the motherless children and made a few scribbled notes in a big leather book.

Dora was glad to be outside again, where they could speak in normal voices. Since Mama had left them no money, Dora announced that they would walk to the fair. This was easier said than done on a nearly empty stomach. She had to carry Tess most of the way. "Just think how wonderful it will be inside," Dora said over and over again to keep her sisters moving around the piles of garbage, the horse carriages, and the open sewer grates. Somehow the trip to the dormitory the day before had seemed to take only a few moments by cable car.

Sweating and exhausted, they arrived at the gate. Dora tried to straighten the front of her dress, which had become rather soiled. They all had only one change of clothes, and somehow she was going to have to figure out how to wash out a few things so they'd at least look presentable.

"Let's go see Mama at her restaurant!" Tess suggested.

"Not yet," Dora said. "Let's give her a little time first. Ready to go in?" Already a crowd had formed outside the gate. Dora couldn't help feeling a bit nervous. The last time they'd come they'd been there with Mama. Dora was afraid that she'd forget where they'd walked and how they'd gotten back.

"Come on!" Phoebe said excitedly. She took her pass from her pocket. Dora found Tess's and her own. But when Lillian plunged her hand in her pocket, she shrieked with distress.

"What's wrong?" Phoebe demanded.

"I forgot it. Or maybe I lost it," Lillian said and began sobbing loudly.

The people around them looked alarmed by Lillian's loud wails. A few of the grown-ups seemed to pretend the brokenhearted girl wasn't there. Finally, a man with a fine, soft derby leaned over and asked, "Little girl, what's the matter?"

"I forgot my fair pass and now I can't go in with my dear sisters and I will miss seeing all the treasures of the world," Lillian replied. She pounded her pretty forehead with her fist and moaned. "And how I wanted to go to the fair!"

"Well, my dear," the man said kindly, "there's no reason for distress. Your ticket is probably misplaced somewhere at your home."

"We have no home!" Lillian sobbed even louder.

Dora and Phoebe exchanged nervous, embarrassed glances. The man in the derby looked unnerved as well. People in line were watching them. Perhaps they even thought he might be saying something to cause the poor, pretty little girl to cry. Quickly, the man removed his wallet and handed Lillian a dollar. "Here, my dear. That's more than enough for your admission," he said and hurried back to join his pale, thin wife.

Dora gave her sister a jab with one elbow. "Thank you, sir," Lillian called back. The crowd, who had been watching the little drama, sent up a little riffle of applause. The man in the derby blushed. "Let's get at the end of the line," Lillian hissed to her sisters.

Suspicious, Dora followed her. By the time they reached the ticket taker, her worst fears were confirmed. "Oh, look!" Lillian said and pulled the green fair pass from her pocket. "I had it all along. Silly me!" She slipped the dollar into her pocket.

"Wait a minute, Lillian," Dora said as they were all ushered through the gate. "You must give that dollar back."

"You're absolutely right," Lillian replied. She scanned the crowd—a sea of identical derbies. "Where do you think he's gone?"

Dora sighed. She knew they'd never find the

man again. She had been so humiliated by her sister's scene that she'd refused to look at his face. Now she couldn't remember anything about what he looked like. Not only was her sister becoming a clever actress but she was also turning into a flim-flam. "That was a despicable trick you just played on that gentleman," Dora announced.

"Lillian," Phoebe added testily, "I bet you did that on purpose to get money for the Ferris wheel."

"Maybe," Lillian replied in a mysterious voice. "He looked rich enough to spare a dollar."

Dora fumed. "That was wrong. Very wrong."

Lillian sighed. She looked contrite. "All right. Buy everyone something to eat." She handed Dora the dollar. "Take it."

The girls purchased overpriced bananas and sweet buns from a vendor. They sat beside the reflecting pool and ate their breakfast, which they washed down with free water from the Hygia tent. Everyone felt much better after that. "Where to first?" Phoebe said eagerly.

But before they could go even a few more steps, a young man in a flat cap rolling a huge wicker armchair on wheels came whizzing up to them. "Hello," he said. "Name's Ben Logan. Need a ride?"

Dora and her sisters looked in amazement at

the young man with the fancy flat cap and coat with brass buttons. Was this some kind of joke? "We don't have any money," Dora said. She gave her sisters a secret warning look, as if to not say another word. He might be crazy.

"Where'd you get the chair?" Lillian demanded. She inspected the wheels, which turned in all directions.

"Columbia Rolling Chair Company. I give tours. Forty cents an hour or you can pay six dollars for a whole day's ride," Ben replied. "It will be an extremely educational endeavor, I can assure you."

"Six dollars!" Dora said and laughed. "Sounds like robbery to me."

Ben grinned. He wasn't very tall or robust. Dora wondered how he could push a chair with a big heavy woman, like the one she'd seen early that morning complaining at the dormitory.

"Sorry, we're not interested. I'm saving my money for the Ferris wheel," Lillian said. She took Tess's grubby hand and began to walk away.

"Wait!" Ben said. He pushed his hat back on his head and scratched his dark, wavy hair. "I wasn't exactly telling the truth. You see, this is my first day with the Columbia Rolling Chair Company. You're my very first customers. I have the whole tour worked out. But I need a rehearsal. And I was wondering if maybe you girls would do me the honor of sitting in this chair so I can acquire necessary practice. The tour will be free, of course."

"All of us?" Lillian said with disdain. She inspected the chair. It was designed for one very large, very fat, grown-up. What would it look like if all four of them squeezed in? Certainly not the elegant impression Lillian Lucille Marie Pomeroy wanted to make.

"Let's try it," Dora said. She liked his smile. She wanted to hear him talk. He sounded so smart. She bet he knew hundreds of spelling words. "I'll hold Phoebe on my lap. Lillian, you hold Tess."

Phoebe did not like the babyish idea of sitting in her older sister's lap, but she was entranced enough by the idea of rolling along at top speed to do as she was told. In a few moments, they were sailing down the broad avenue with the wind in their faces.

"You're pretty strong," Lillian shouted approvingly at Ben.

Ben laughed. "I'm pushing this chair to make my way through college. It's a summer job," he said and then cleared his throat and began in a very serious voice. "On our right we see the long, elegant sweep of the Manufactures Building extending all the way down to the Peristyle. On the very right we see the Chocolate-Menier Building."

"What's that smell?" Phoebe said.

"Chocolate, stupid," Lillian hissed.

"Stop! Stop! Is this the place with the gigantic chocolate Venus?" Phoebe demanded.

Ben stopped the chair. He looked puzzled. "I haven't heard of a chocolate Venus," he said. "Sorry. Perhaps I need to do more research. May I continue?"

"She weighs tons!" Phoebe said in a helpful voice. "You better find out about her. People want to know about stuff like that, even if they can't have a taste." She gave Lillian an accusing look.

"Thank you," Ben said politely. Dora could hear a tone of amusement in his voice. "May I continue? The Mines Building is three hundred and fifty by seven hundred feet long, and the Electricity Building nearly the same."

"Watch out!" Lillian called. At the last minute, Ben swerved the chair and just missed colliding with an old woman armed with a parasol.

"The Mines Building was inspired by the Italian Renaissance, but the exterior has a French spirit to it. The second floor galleries are sixty feet wide."

"Boring, boring, boring," Lillian whispered to her sisters.

Ben coughed nervously. "Would you like to see the Liberty Bell?"

The girls nodded. Tess was snoring. Ben pushed them through a crowd of sightseers outside the enormous Administration Building. In front of the door was a Liberty Bell on a steady oak frame with an American flag unfurled in one corner.

"What's so great about this bell?" Lillian demanded.

"This is actually a replica of the famous bell that was hung in 1753 in the Pennsylvania State House, which later became Independence Hall. As you can see, it is inscribed with the words, 'Proclaim Liberty Throughout the Land.' It has been rung every Fourth of July since 1776 to commemorate the signing of the Declaration of Independence. In 1846 the bell developed a crack."

"Too bad," Lillian said. "Can we see the Ferris wheel now?"

"I'm not finished," Ben said. His voice sounded disturbed. He took a deep breath. "The bell continues to symbolize unity and celebration."

"Do you know how to get to the Streets of Cairo?" Lillian demanded.

"I think educational displays are more appropriate for young ladies like yourselves," he said, frowning. "There are lots of pickpockets and savages over in the Midway Plaisance area."

Lillian raised one eyebrow. That sounded a lot more interesting than Liberty Bells.

"And notice the sculpture to the left of the Administration Building door. It is called *Earth*," Ben continued. "The other sculptures are called *Fire, Water,* and *Air.*"

"What happened to *Earth*'s trousers?" Phoebe demanded and muffled a laugh.

"Let's continue with the tour," Ben said hurriedly. He swung the chair around and trotted full-speed past the east facade of the Administration Building, past the statue of Benjamin Franklin about to be electrocuted by lightning with his kite, past giggling women with lunch baskets. "Here's something I know you'll enjoy," he said, out of breath. "It's the Edison Company's electric fountain that shoots colored streams of sparkling water gaily into the air." He stopped the tour to mop the back of his neck with a handkerchief.

The girls ignored the electric fountain. Instead they were fascinated by another fountain that featured an amazing boat. It carried stone paddlers with fancy oars and people pointing and water squirting everywhere. The statues had such stern, serious faces. All around the fountain were swimming horses and splashing babies who really did not seem to go with the serious people. It looked to Dora like the fanciest boat ride on earth.

"Who's sitting in the chair on top?" Lillian demanded, pointing up at the great ship.

"Her name is Columbia. She is supposed to symbolize our country," Ben said in a weary voice. "The fountain represents a long voyage on uncharted waters. Our country going through turbulent waves of time."

Lillian shook her head. "I don't know if Mrs. Columbia could get across the Platte River in that crazy boat. Look at those wild horses swimming in front. And why are all those stone babies crawling around with bunches of leaves and fruit?"

Her sisters burst into laughter.

"It's an allegory," Ben said, his face turning bright red. "The Columbian Fountain was designed by Frederick William MacMonnies, and it's very famous."

"I think it's beautiful," Dora said. She could tell that their tour guide was losing his composure. She liked Ben. She liked the color of his eyes. She liked the word *allegory.* She wondered how to spell it. What difference did it make if what he'd told them was incredibly boring? Her sisters were rude. They were always ruining everything.

"Take a look at those wild animals!" Lillian said, pointing to the life-size elk and bears made of gleaming marble. While she jumped out of the rolling chair and hurried to inspect the creatures, she noticed people on the other side of the Columbian Fountain throwing something over their right shoulders with their backs to the water.

"What are they doing?" Phoebe asked Ben.

"Making wishes, I suppose. A silly waste of money," Ben said in an impatient voice. "Now, where was I?"

"Do the wishes come true?" Phoebe asked. Now here was something valuable to know about.

"I don't really know," Ben replied. "As I was saying, the Manufactures Building is seven hundred sixty-seven feet wide and one thousand six hundred eighty-seven feet long, making it nearly thirty-one acres. The colossal structure was designed by George Post of New York. You girls should go inside and take the elevator to the top of the promenade on the roof. Best view at the fair."

Dora sighed as the chair rolled along. She wondered if she would ever be able to go back to school. Maybe one day she could get a good job like this and make enough money to go to college.

". . . On top of the Music Hall," Ben droned on and on, "is the magnificent sculpture by Daniel Chester French, of Columbus driving a four-horse chariot."

"I thought he was a sailor. What's he doing with horses?" Phoebe demanded.

"It's symbolic. Purely symbolic," Ben said. His voice rose angrily. Sheepishly, Lillian climbed back into the chair. "Would you like to see the other side of the Manufactures Building?" Ben began to push harder and faster. Dora had the horrible feeling he might swerve and send them flying into the canal.

"This is fun!" Lillian said with delight. "Look at the boats with the pretty striped tops. When I'm rich and famous I'm going to buy one of those."

"There are forty electric launches available for rides," Ben said in a breathless voice. "The gondoliers are dressed in bright costumes."

"What's a gondolier?" Phoebe demanded.

"The fellow who paddles and steers the boat," Ben said wearily.

"Oh," Phoebe said. "Just like Columbus *and* Mrs. Columbia. Do you suppose they're married?"

Lillian shrugged. Dora rolled her eyes.

By the time they made it to the end of the building, Ben was pushing the chair more and more slowly. Finally, the chair stopped.

"What's wrong?" Dora asked.

"End of tour," Ben said. He gave a little bow. His face was bright red, and his fancy jacket was stained with sweat. "What did you think? Be honest."

Tess woke up and slipped from Lillian's arms. She trotted toward the canal in pursuit of a duck. "It was wonderful," Dora said and ran to retrieve her sister before she plummeted into the water.

"You want my honest opinion?" Lillian said.

Ben nodded.

"It was very boring. Except for the wishing fountain. I liked that," Lillian admitted.

Ben frowned. "I guess I need to work on the more dramatic material." He sighed. "Some of the other fair vendors make fun of us. They call us the 'gospel chariots.' They criticize us for sounding too bookish."

"Tell about the fierce lions and elephants and the sword dancers," Phoebe suggested in her wisest voice. "People want to know about that kind of thing. It's exciting."

Ben tipped his hat again. "Thanks for the review. Do you girls know your way? You can't be too careful about pickpockets. See those fellows over there by the bridge?"

The girls nodded. There were three or four men in uniforms. "Those are the Columbian guards. They keep order. They look out for unruly types. If you ever need help, go to them." A group of ladies wearing bright blue badges walked past. "And those are the women from the Travelers' Aid Society. They help spot the sinful. And then of course there are the secret policemen."

"Secret?" Lillian said nervously.

"They are officers specially trained in detecting the thieves and sharpers of all descriptions that might gravitate to the fair."

Ben's information impressed Phoebe, but it made Lillian nervous. She thought about the dollar she'd gotten from the man at the entrance gate that morning. She'd pay him back if she had the money. "You know where we could get some jobs around here?" Lillian asked.

Ben looked at her with surprise. "Nice young ladies like you? I thought you were here on vacation. Where are your parents?"

"Mama's an actress but she's working as a waitress temporarily at the Women's Building. Da's across the way at the Wild West Show," Lillian said proudly.

Ben frowned. "Your parents are in the theatre?"

Lillian and Phoebe nodded. Dora, who had rejoined them, kept her mouth shut. She could tell that Ben did not approve.

"That's a sinful profession," he said in a haughty voice.

The girls looked confused. They had heard theatre called many things, but never a profession. What was that? "I must take you back to a safe, responsible institution. I cannot leave you here," Ben said. His voice sounded cold, as if he condemned Da and Mama and everyone connected with theatre everywhere. "I'll take you back to the Children's Building. It's right next to the Women's Building. Perhaps you can find something constructive and wholesome to do with your time there."

He did not add another bit of information the whole way back, even though they passed some rather fascinating, wild-looking islands and bridges and trees that Lillian secretly considered exploring. When they finally arrived at the Children's Building, Ben pointed and said, "And when you're through in here, go immediately to your mother in the restaurant. Do not speak to any strangers. If you are confronted by a solicitor, say no and quickly walk away until you are out of their reach."

Dora thanked Ben. "Good-bye," Dora said, wondering if she'd ever see him again.

"Good luck," Lillian and Phoebe said. They waved as Ben scurried out of sight with his rolling chair.

"You gotta red face, Dorie," Tess said as she took her big sister's hand.

Chapter

6

"Come and see the babies!"

"Here is where they check the babies!"

A group of boys, perhaps ten years old, called to the crowd of visitors milling about in a smaller white building beside the Women's Building. "What's going on?" Lillian asked. "Let's go see."

"I don't think you should," Dora said warily. "You remember what Ben said. These boys could be sharpers."

"They don't look old enough," Phoebe said. She and her sisters wandered closer to the two-story white building decorated with flags and medallions showing children in odd costumes. There was a blue frieze and words carved above the arched door. "What's it say, Dora?" Phoebe asked.

" 'The hope of the world is in the children,' " Dora replied, dragging Tess by the hand.

Suddenly, the group of boys quickly surrounded them. "Go see the babies," said a small, thin fellow with a thatch of greasy blond hair. He had the face of an old man.

"What do the babies do?" Lillian demanded.

The boy winked. "They fly. They sing. They dance."

Lillian frowned and put her hands on her waist. "Babies don't do anything but cry and get into trouble," she said.

The boy and his two companions laughed heartily and slapped their legs. "Don't tell our boss that," the blond boy said.

"You get paid to stand out here shouting at people?" Lillian asked, intrigued.

The blond boy nodded. "There's plenty of money to be made at the fair." Then he added in a low voice, "You can work for us, too, you know."

Lillian's eyes sparkled.

"We aren't interested," Dora said. She grabbed Lillian by the elbow and hauled her toward the doorway of the Children's Building. Phoebe and Tess followed them. "That boy's a rascal. Stay away from him," Dora warned Lillian.

Lillian shook her older sister's hand free. "You

think you know everything. I bet I could make some money for the Ferris wheel."

"Come on!" Phoebe called to them. She was several yards ahead and was motioning to them excitedly with her hand. Children's voices and laughter and shouting echoed inside. She and her sisters followed the noise and discovered in the center of the building an open courtyard with a railing on all four sides. Inside the courtyard children swung on trapezes, balanced on parallel bars, and leapt over bulky objects that looked like horses with no heads. Two girls squealed with delight as they twirled from rings hanging from the tall ceiling. A group of boys flipped Indian clubs and wands. Grown-ups watched from the galleries above.

"What is this?" Phoebe asked eagerly.

Dora pointed to a sign and read aloud, "Equipment donated by North American Turner Bund to make children strong and healthy, agile and courageous, keen, resolute and of cheerful disposition, graceful and perfect physically."

For several moments the girls watched the other children laughing and shoving each other from the parallel bars. "How'd they get in there?" Lillian asked. "Think they were invited?"

"I just saw somebody walk right in. Looks like it's free," Phoebe said. "Too scary for me, though."

Tess wriggled from Dora's arms. She hooked her hands on the railing and swung her fat legs out the way she saw the older girls doing in the courtyard area.

"Nice place for an audience," Lillian said, glancing up at the adults looking down from the gallery. Without waiting for Dora's permission, Lillian ducked under the railing and got in line for the trapeze.

"What a show-off," Phoebe murmured. Dora nodded.

Tess began screaming. "Me. I wanna go with Lillian!"

The nearby grown-ups frowned, as if Tess did not belong among children who were courageous, keen, resolute, and of cheerful disposition.

"Hush, Little Kisses! You're not big enough," Dora said.

This only made Tess howl louder.

"Let's go upstairs," Phoebe suggested in an effort to distract Tess. "I want to see where they store the babies those boys were talking about."

Dora, Tess, and Phoebe climbed the steps and discovered, on the second floor of the southeast corner, a curious room with a sign over it that said, KITCHEN GARDEN. Another group of amused grown-ups stood beside a large window and were peering in and making approving comments.

Dora and Phoebe were curious. They dragged Tess down the hallway and peered in, too. On the other side of the glass window was a curious sight. Twenty-five girls exactly Phoebe's age were wearing white muslin caps and aprons. On their shoulders were pinned little badges showing a miniature knife, fork, and spoon tied with a ribbon. Some of the girls swept with little brooms. Others washed dishes or scrubbed clothes with little scrub boards. Half a dozen were busy messing up a row of tiny beds. When they were through rumpling the sheets and blankets, they began to make the beds.

"What are they doing?" Dora asked, perplexed.

"Shshshsh!" said the man next to her, who was smiling and leaning closer to the glass.

Dora found the girls with caps very odd. She made beds every day, but that was because someone had slept in them. She couldn't imagine messing up a bed for no good reason except to make it again.

Gracefully, the girls turned the mattresses and punched them. They spread the sheets with the hems turned in a precise fashion, then they covered the bed with a blanket. In unison they folded and tucked the blanket under the mattress. Meanwhile, the sweepers, who had emptied the corners of invisible dust, pushed up their pretty sleeves and carried miniature buckets. On their hands and knees they used scrub brushes and washed the floor.

"O dear what can the matter be, Cook has forgotten the salt!" the cheerful girls sang together, accompanied by the tinny music of a hidden piano. The perfect little housekeepers were so absorbed in their chores that they seemed completely unaware of the charmed grown-ups on the other side of the glass.

"Doesn't look like a bit of fun to me," Dora murmured. She wondered if it was some kind of trick. Perhaps the girls with the caps were enchanted. She had never seen anything so ridiculous in her life.

"Oh," Phoebe said with her forehead pressed against the glass. "I wish I could do that."

"Why?" Dora asked. "You can do chores at home every day."

Phoebe shook her head. "But not like this," she said softly, admiring the order and cleanliness. The other side of the glass represented everything Phoebe's life wasn't—calm, predictable, respectable. She was certain these happy girls lived in real houses with happy, normal mothers and fathers. They had breakfast every morning and nutritious dinners every night. Their clothes were bleached clean and pressed carefully. Their shoes were shined, and they always had fresh ribbons in their combed hair before they went to school.

They didn't live in the back of crowded wagons or dirty tenements or noisy boarding houses. They didn't have to scrounge for food or nap among the scenery behind stage in drafty theaters waiting for their mothers and fathers to remember where they were. These happy girls in their caps and aprons and special wondrous pins were so lucky. "How did they get in there?" Phoebe wondered aloud.

The man standing next to her pointed to a woman sitting in the corner. She had her hair in a tight topknot that made her thin face look even thinner. "You want to be in the Broom Brigade you have to see Miss Larrabee. She signed up my daughter, Maizie. See her? She's the one with the braids." He smiled proudly.

Phoebe sighed. "The Broom Brigade. Does it cost much, sir?"

The man shook his head. "Doesn't cost anything. Miss Larrabee gets parents' permission, and then they do a little training session. All for free."

"Free?" Phoebe said in amazement.

"And when they're finished, they get a snack and then they can do woodworking or model clay or play in a room filled with toys or they can read books in the library."

This sounded too marvelous to be true. Before Dora could stop Phoebe, her sister marched around the corner to the door, knocked, and begged to become part of the Broom Brigade.

"I'll do anything. I'm a hard worker," Phoebe said eagerly. Miss Larrabee stood in the doorway, looking surprised.

"What are you doing?" Dora hissed and tried to pull her sister away. Tess had escaped down the hallway. Dora had no time for Phoebe's foolishness.

Miss Larrabee smiled. "I'm delighted to hear that. I presume you have your parents' permission."

"Yes, yes," Phoebe said hurriedly before Dora could interrupt. "Can I wear one of those pins and one of those caps and gowns, too?" She licked her lips.

"Certainly. Is this your sister?" Miss Larrabee said. She smiled in a way that made Dora wilt. She was certain Miss Larrabee was examining her dirty dress, mussed hair, falling-down stockings, and scuffed shoes.

"No . . . no, she isn't," Phoebe stammered. "I mean, yes, she is. When can I start?"

"Today, if you like." Miss Larrabee opened the door wide and let Phoebe in. Before she closed it, she turned to Dora and said, "We finish at five o'clock today, if you'd care to join us."

"No, thank you, ma'am," Dora said quickly. "I'll come and pick her up." She was afraid of being bewitched like her sister. She backed up. "I have to . . . I have to take care of my other little sister."

"All right then, we'll see you at five o'clock." The door shut.

Desperately, Dora turned and ran down the hall in search of Tess. One by one her whole family was vanishing right before her eyes—first Da at the Wild West Show, then Ma at the restaurant. Lillian had disappeared in the gymnastic equipment area, and Phoebe had been swallowed up by a kitchen. What if she couldn't find Tess? Dora broke into a sweat and ran as fast as she could through the crowd.

Somehow her youngest sister had scrambled down the steps and was trying to crawl under some grown-up legs. Just like at the gymnastics area and the kitchen, there were grown-ups peering in the window hole at a vast nursery lined with baby cribs and cradles and heaps of toys. Dora wondered where all the children had come from. Had they been lost by their parents at the fair?

Did the police bring them here, some kind of lost and found?

A door opened. The noise was tremendous. It sounded like a million shouting, crying children. Tess wriggled through the jungle of legs and scampered into the nursery. The noise did not bother Tess. She knew what she wanted.

Toys.

Strewn all about the room was the most marvelous collection of dolls and tops and balls. Nursemaids in striped uniforms and aprons carried yelping, yodeling babies. Toddlers trundled past. Tess boldly pushed her way to the center of the pile. No one even noticed Tess's daring break-in until Dora burst into the room and tried to pull her sister away. "You can't stay here," Dora warned. She grabbed her sister and tugged. Stubborn Tess would have none of it. She had found paradise and this was where she intended to stay. She let out a bloodcurdling howl.

"What's the problem here? This little girl doesn't have a claim check," one of the nursemaids told Dora. "Can't leave without a claim check."

"What's a claim check?" Dora said, growing more terrified by the minute.

"A number pinned to her back. Every child gets

one. The parent takes the other stub. That's how we know who the child belongs to."

Tess screamed louder. "I came for my sister," Dora bellowed. "She snuck in here when the door opened. It was an accident. She's not supposed to be here."

"I see," the nursemaid said. She had a pinched, tired expression. "Take her away, please."

Dora hauled her sister out of the play area by her armpits. Tess struggled with demonic fury, but she was no match for Dora. "We have to go see Mama," Dora kept repeating, hoping this would work some miracle. Tess didn't care if she ever saw her mother again. She wanted to play with those toys.

"Come on!" Dora cried with frustration. With her kicking, hollering sister under one arm, she managed to find Lillian among the gymnastic equipment.

"I've got a job," Lillian said triumphantly. "I get to sprinkle water on the floor and pick up trash in the gymnasium area." She pulled four dull-colored pennies from her pocket. "And see how much I've already made? The children turn upside down and they lose their pocket change. Finders keepers, losers weepers."

"But it's not your money," Dora reminded her above Tess's squalls.

Lillian waved her hand dismissively. "My boss told me I was to clean up. That's what I'm doing. No one said anything about returning lost coins."

Dora groaned. She could feel the ground shifting underneath her feet. Everything was changing. Lillian was heading for a life of crime. Phoebe had been enchanted by a bizarre housekeeping religion. And her youngest sister was determined to deafen Dora until she checked her into a baby corral. "Shut up!" Dora finally shouted at Tess.

"That is not the proper way to silence an impressionable young child," a frowning, stout woman with a badge said. "Try using the kind of discipline that ensures good manners, good morals, and the kindly development of the child's natural powers." Then she handed Dora a leaflet for a lecture entitled "The Kindergarten As Character Builder."

Tess was so surprised by the stranger's commanding speech that her mouth snapped shut.

"Thank you," Dora said in a small voice. She tucked the leaflet under her arm and slunk away with silent Tess and Lillian in tow. When they were out of sight of the woman, Tess demonstrated the development of her natural powers by sticking her tongue out at her eldest sister.

Dora ignored her. They had to get out of this

place. "Lillian, we have to rescue Phoebe. Then we'll go see Mama. We'll have a nice meal," Dora said as confidently as she could. "And then we'll all go home together."

"I'd rather stay here forever," Lillian grumbled as they trudged up the steps to the second floor Kitchen Garden to find Phoebe.

Once the sisters had found each other again, they headed to the neighboring Women's Building. At the top floor was the crowded Roof Garden Cafe. Neither Dora nor the other girls had expected such a crowd. The place was packed. Dora jumped up and down trying to spot Mama. At last she saw her and felt relieved that she had not been fired for arriving late for work that morning. Mama's face was flushed, and her hair was coming out of her white cap. Phoebe waved. Lillian called.

Mama looked up and saw them. She seemed determined to put on a brave face and signaled for them to take a stool next to a low counter. The other people around them, who had obviously been waiting in line for some time, did not look pleased.

"Draw one in the dark!" one of the waitresses shouted to the cook, who poured a cup of black coffee and thumped it on the pass-through window.

"What else you got?" the red-faced cook demanded.

"Slaughter in the pan and white wings," the waitress said.

Dora and her sister watched in amazement, wondering what this meant. After a few minutes, the cook slid a plate of steak and two poached eggs out through the window.

"What are you doing here?" Mama said nervously. She stood beside the girls with her special pad of paper and pencil.

"We came to see you," Phoebe said. Mama frowned. Phoebe felt hurt that she was not pleased to see them.

"You got to order something. My boss is watching," Mama said. "Look at the menu. I got a million customers. My feet are killing me."

"Ham sandwich," Lillian said.

"Me, too," Phoebe added. It seemed so strange to give Mama food orders. She never cooked at home if she could avoid it.

"How we going to pay for this?" Dora asked in a worried voice.

"I got some fees," Mama said, referring to the tips in her pocket. "What'll you have, Dora? That lunch cutter behind the counter slices the meat so thin it's practically transparent. And don't order anything with a tomato. Found a worm in one this afternoon."

"I'll have a fried egg sandwich," Dora said. "So will Tess."

"No," Tess whined. "I want slaughter in the pan."

"It's too expensive," Dora hissed. "Order something else."

"Cheese," Tess said. "Yellow cheese."

Mama made a few quick notes and trotted away. She handed the check to the cook. "Try not to break nothing this time, will ya?" he said in a nasty voice.

"You better not charge me twenty-five cents for that one-penny butter dish," Mama grumbled. Then she turned and said something the girls couldn't hear.

"The men eat with their hats on," Lillian observed. "They don't have any napkins like the restaurant we went to with Da."

Phoebe wasn't listening. She cocked her ear toward the family at a nearby table. Two girls, a boy, a mother, and a father. They looked like well-dressed tourists. As they ate they smiled and chatted. Their father leaned forward to listen carefully to what each of his children was saying. He laughed. They all laughed. Phoebe wondered what was so funny. She thought of Da, and she missed his silly jokes. She watched the tourist mother carefully cut the littlest girl's meat into tiny pieces. Mama never did that.

At that moment Phoebe realized how completely different her life was compared to the children in this other family. She understood that she and her sisters and parents might never enjoy each other's company on a special holiday like this. And she felt very, very sad.

"What's the matter, Phoebe?" Dora asked.

"Nothing," Phoebe replied. Suddenly, she did not feel the least bit hungry.

Chapter

7

The next morning Mama was so exhausted from working a double-shift that she could barely get out of bed to go to work again. She stumbled around the room and dressed without saying much of anything to the girls, who stayed under their covers so they wouldn't get in her way. "There are a few rolls I brought from the restaurant," Mama told Dora as she pinned up her hair. "They were stale and they were going to throw them out, but they let me keep them. You can eat those."

"When we gonna see Da?" Tess demanded and fed a few crumbs to Nancy.

"Lord knows," Mama said and sighed. "We got to make some money, Little Kisses, or we aren't going to have any place to stay in Chicago. Now you be good and do what Dora says."

"Waitressing is only going to be for a little while, Mama," Lillian said in an encouraging voice. "Once we get our feet back on the ground. Then I'll bet you can audition. Buffalo Bill will come around. Just you wait and see."

Mama did not even crack a smile. She just looked at Lillian with a dull, vacant expression. "You sure got your daddy's ever-hopeful streak," Mama said and shook her head. She kissed each of her daughters on the cheek and shut the door behind herself.

"Didn't even get to tell her about the Broom Brigade," Phoebe said. She held her knees up to her chin. She looked very small in the middle of the big bed. "Didn't even get to ask her to sign the paper."

"She'll sign it, don't worry," Dora said in a bright voice. Mama's smile, which they remembered from the train, was gone. All her optimism and her energy seemed to have vanished as well. Everything about Mama reminded Dora of the way she'd been on the ranch. Silent and sad and restless. It wasn't a good sign. "Come on, lazybones!" Dora said and clapped her hands together. "You got to get to work, too!"

The girls quickly dressed. Dora had washed their stockings out in the basin the night before, and they were still slightly damp. "These feel cold and clammy!" Lillian complained.

"Too bad," Dora said. "They're clean. Put them on."

"You are too bossy," Phoebe growled. She and Lillian rushed downstairs before all the warm water was gone in the common bathroom.

Tess pouted and refused to cooperate. "What we gonna do, Dorie?" Tess asked her oldest sister. "Huh, Dorie? What we gonna do?"

"We're going to the fair, on the trolley, too," Dora said wearily. She wished she had a job like Phoebe and Lillian—something to do besides baby-sit whiny Tess. "We'll have some fun. Now get dressed."

Tess dressed herself. She gnawed on a roll. When the girls returned, Dora made sure their hair was brushed. She counted the nickels that Mama had left for them. They would use these to take the trolley. "Ready?" Dora said as they hurried out of the dormitory to the street. "You got your fair passes?"

Phoebe, Lillian, and Tess nodded. "Nancy's coming, too. She wants to see the fair," Tess announced.

"She'll get lost," Dora protested. "You remember the last time she got lost under the porch? You wouldn't go to bed without crying for three weeks."

Tess looked up at her sister defiantly. "Nancy wants to go to the fair."

"All right," Dora said reluctantly. "But if anything happens to her, don't blame me."

Dora and her sisters rode the trolley to the fair gates. The sky was bright, and the southeast wind smelled of the lake and open distance. Dora's hair whipped in her face. Phoebe and Lillian smiled broadly. "Our first day at work!" Phoebe said.

"I feel grown up, do you?" Lillian said.

Dora couldn't help feeling a twinge of envy. When they reached the fair entrance and went inside, Lillian turned to Dora and announced in a very superior voice, "We don't need you to walk us to the Children's Building. We know the way very well, thank you, don't we, Phoebe?"

Phoebe nodded. Dora sighed. "All right then. You can walk this once. But remember at five o'clock I'm going to meet you both outside the entrance. There are plenty of clocks. You be on time. What are you going to eat for lunch?"

"They give everyone in the Broom Brigade a nutritious meal," Phoebe said.

"I have my own money to buy something from a vendor," Lillian replied.

"Oh," Dora said, suddenly deflated by the fact that they did not need her wisdom or advice about where to find food. "Be good, both of you."

Phoebe linked arms with Lillian, and the two girls trotted happily away. Dora watched them and wondered what she and Tess were going to do all day with no money. She did not dare bother Mama at the restaurant again. It was still too early to go inside most of the buildings. They walked and walked until they reached the fountain with Columbia in her strange boat. Tess was too tired to go any farther.

"Hungry!" she complained. She sat on the edge of the fountain. "Soda water. Soda water. Soda-soda-soda water!"

As if from nowhere, Dora heard the sound of wheels on the pavement. She turned and, to her complete surprise, saw Ben wheeling toward them with an empty wicker chair. "Hello!" he called to them. "What happened to your two other sisters?"

Dora smiled nervously. "They found jobs at the Children's Building."

"What about you?"

Dora blushed. "I'd like to make some money, but I have to take care of my sister."

"I see. You a pretty good baby-sitter?"

Dora nodded. She hoped that Tess would keep her mouth shut for once.

"Jobs are hard to come by these days," he said in an understanding voice.

Dora bit her lip. "What I really wish is that I could do what you're doing."

"Pushing a chair for the Columbia Rolling Chair Company? I'm afraid you're a bit too young."

Dora stared at her feet. "No, not that. What I mean is—," she paused. She felt like an idiot. Everything she said sounded so stupid. She took a deep breath and blurted, "What I mean is—I'd like to go to college like you. If I had enough money, that's what I'd do."

Ben didn't laugh. He didn't make fun of her. He simply scratched his head in a thoughtful way. "You know," he said, "I had a couple yesterday who said they were looking for someone to watch their little boy for the day. They had not been able to get him into the Children's Building nursery. Maybe they'd hire you instead. I'll tell you that boy's a handful. I'm supposed to meet them at eleven o'clock this morning right under the elk statue. See it over there?"

Dora nodded. "I'd like to watch him," she said, "if they'd pay me."

"Oh, they'd pay you all right. Gave me a dollar tip. They're from Indianapolis and they're fancy folks. Why don't you meet me over there by that statue and I'll talk to them and see if maybe we can't work something out."

Dora was delighted. Ben said good-bye and trotted off to give an old lady a quick ride to the Bureau of Public Comfort. Dora and Tess waited beside the fountain and watched a gondola sail past. And then another. Such a perfect day. While Dora daydreamed about escaping from her family and going far away to college, her little sister ripped up pieces of old newspaper and threw them into the water like little boats.

"Hey, you!" a Columbian guard shouted, startling Dora out of her reverie. "What do you think you're doing? Children aren't supposed to play in the fountains. Don't let me catch her breaking the rules again."

"Sorry," Dora said, wondering what other rules there might be that she didn't know about. She grabbed her sister's hand. She looked around and wondered who else might be watching them. "She won't do it again, sir." Dora stood up and took Tess's hand. They started walking away from the man with the uniform. Right away Tess found a button and a hair pin. She was good at finding little things. She didn't care about the nine-foot red-wood tree exhibit or the postage stamp display in the Government Building.

By the time they'd walked around for a few minutes inside the building, it was time to walk back. Dora didn't want to be late. She worried that Ben might take the couple from Indianapolis and leave without her if she wasn't on time.

In the distance, beyond a fierce polar bear statue, Dora saw Ben pushing a woman in a practical, wide-brimmed hat. She sat like a queen, with a basket in her lap. Her husband, in a dark derby and wire-rim glasses, led a little boy by his hand. Ben waved. Dora waved back. "Come on. And be good," she said to Tess between clenched teeth.

"I am good, Dorie," Tess said and pouted.

"This is Mr. and Mrs. Thaw," Ben said. "And their son, Wilbur."

Wilbur was a fat little boy with pale eyelashes and pale eyebrows. His suspicious gray eyes were heavy-lidded, like a snapping turtle's. He squished up his features and bared his teeth.

"Isn't he the cutest little thing!" Mrs. Thaw said.

Dora nodded nervously. "My name's Dora, and this is my little sister Tess. She's four. How old are you, Wilbur?"

Wilbur growled.

Mrs. Thaw handed Dora a large, heavy basket. "Wilbur is on a very special diet. I only allow him to eat certain foods—all healthful. Please make sure he finishes everything. He's such a delicate child. Worries me to death." She smiled adoringly at her young son, who was busy scuffing the toes of his shining leather shoes on the sharp gravel.

"We'll meet you back here at four o'clock sharp," Mr. Thaw said. He had a cold, fishy face, and when he spoke his nose made little whistling noises. "Do not be late. We want Wilbur to be exposed only to educational exhibits—the Fisheries Building, the Weather Bureau, the Manufactures Building. He loves trains, don't you, Wilbur? You may take him to the Transportation Building."

Wilbur made some noises that his parents claimed sounded precisely like a locomotive. They applauded. Dora would have tried to clap, too, except that she had to hold the heavy picnic basket. Secretly, she wondered if Wilbur was actually making the sounds of a man-eating tiger.

"Do not, I repeat, do not take him to such immoral places as the Midway Plaisance," Mrs. Thaw said and fluttered her handkerchief. "Am I understood?"

"We'll pay you one dollar," Mr. Thaw said, "that

is, if you do a good job. Wilbur hasn't many play-mates." He looked skeptically at dirty Tess, who was chewing a strand of hair. "This might be a good chance for him to learn some valuable social skills."

"Good-bye, my darling, " Mrs. Thaw called.

Dora hardly heard a word they said. She was so thrilled by the idea of making a whole dollar — more money than she'd ever made in her life. She could take her sisters out to dinner. She could help Mama pay the rent. There were so many things she could do with a dollar.

She watched Mrs. Thaw rolling away in the chair with her husband trotting dutifully beside her. Ben turned and winked at her over his shoulder. That wink alone was worth all the trouble of taking care of Wilbur, Dora decided. That wink was worth even more than a dollar. "Well," Dora announced, "I think we'll go to the Transportation Building. What about it, Wilbur?"

Wilbur did not answer. He marched up to Tess, grabbed Nancy by her one good arm, and scampered to the Columbian Fountain. "Stop!" Tess cried, too shocked at first to speak. "Get her, Dorie. Get her!"

"Come back, Wilbur!" Dora ran as fast as she could, but Wilbur was very quick even though he had such fat, stumpy legs. Expertly, he ran to the fountain and held poor, old Nancy under water until she was good and drowned. Tess burst into inconsolable tears.

"Nancy!" Tess cried.

Dora grabbed the doll. But Wilbur held tight. There was a terrible tearing sound. "Her arm!" Tess screamed. "He killed her arm!"

Wilbur smiled so that his fangs showed. He held the amputated arm in his fist like a prize, but before Dora could snatch it, he pitched the poor arm as far as he could. It landed out of reach near one of the spouting water monsters.

Tess shrieked. "Wilbur!" Dora screamed. How was she going to get the arm back? Poor, feeble Nancy, an invalid, hung limply by one leg. Wilbur thought this was quite amusing and was about to lunge for her again when Dora caught him tightly by the collar of his sailor suit and held him out of reach. "You nasty creature!" she said in his ear. "You touch this doll again and I'll feed you to a lion. Do you understand?"

Wilbur looked up at her with glowering eyes, as if the idea intrigued him. He clenched his jaw, but he did not speak. Dora held Wilbur in one hand and Tess and Nancy in the other, far enough apart so that they couldn't hurt one another. Helplessly, she watched the little white arm bob farther and farther away.

"What's the problem here?" the Columbian guard demanded. "I thought I told you to keep little rogues out of the water."

"I'm sorry, sir, this is an emergency. My sister's doll's arm has been thrown out there and I can't get it back. That appendage is very precious and she's quite inconsolable." Dora used as many difficult spelling words as she could remember. Some grown-ups were easily impressed.

"I see," the Columbian guard said. He peered out into the fountain. He signaled to another guard, who signaled to another guard. Pretty soon there were four Columbian guards with a long pole fishing about in the Columbian Fountain. When they caught the little, white, soggy arm, Dora would have burst into applause except for the fact that she had to hold on to Wilbur's collar very tightly so that he wouldn't bite anyone. "Thank you. Thank you so much!" Dora exclaimed. She tucked the soggy arm in her pocket, and she carefully hid Nancy in the picnic basket for safekeeping. "Come along, children," she announced.

Dora took Wilbur and Tess past the Administration Building and the Mines Building. The walk took so long that she didn't think they could visit the Transportation Building without a rest. She found a grassy spot near one of the lagoons and lowered the heavy picnic basket. They'd eat lunch, she decided. That was something to do. And when they were finished, the basket would be much lighter.

"Sit here," Dora ordered. She had to watch Wilbur carefully so that he did not get too close to Tess. Tess was no fool. She stayed as far away from the toothy boy as she could. "Now, what do we have here?" Dora said and opened the basket. She discovered a glass jar of carrots, three hard-boiled eggs, some hard, brown crackers, a tin of wilted lettuce, a little pouch of wheat germ, a glass bottle of milk, and two very bruised apples. "Wilbur, your mother said you should eat all this. I don't see how you can."

When Wilbur refused to eat one bite, Dora and Tess did not let the picnic go to waste. They gobbled up everything but the wheat germ and the hard, dry, tasteless crackers—which they fed to the ducks. "You're going to be hungry, Wilbur," Dora said, though she secretly doubted that he needed the food. Wilbur's heavy stomach jiggled up and down as he busily stamped on ants on the pavement. This kept him amused for several minutes.

Dora spent the rest of the afternoon chasing Wilbur from one danger to the next. He tried to climb over the edge of the bridge as he raced out onto the Wooded Island. He tore around and around the Japanese Ho-o-den Temple. He broke tree branches and hunted squirrels. Dora had hoped that being among the trees and bushes of the peaceful little island might put Wilbur in a better mood. Instead he became wilder and more ferocious. He terrorized the other tourists until they complained and a Columbian guard asked Dora and the children to go elsewhere.

Dora wondered what time it was. How would she ever survive until four o'clock? Even a whole dollar was hardly worth this torture. "Tired," Tess complained as they walked past a lovely rose garden.

"Wilbur!" Dora said. "Come sit down here in the shade for a moment." She fanned herself with one of the maps she had found on the ground. She wanted to make sure she'd be able to find her way back to Mr. and Mrs. Thaw. She leaned against a tree. The afternoon was growing hotter by the minute. Wilbur galloped around a soda water vendor. He had no intention of slowing down even for a moment. "Wilbur," she called louder, "I'll tell you a story if you come and sit down."

He paused and looked at her with squinty, suspicious eyes.

"I'll tell you a story about a lion," she promised.

He came closer. Cleverly, she directed him to sit on the other side of her, away from poor Tess. Wilbur sat down and directed his complete attention to Dora as she made up a very long, very boring story told in a monotonous voice she had perfected after years of putting her younger sisters to sleep at night. It wasn't long before Wilbur was curled up and snoring. Tess leaned against her sister and went right to sleep.

A great wave of exhaustion swept over Dora. And before she knew it, she was asleep, too. She dreamt she was racing across the fields in Nebraska. She was running because she was late for school. To her amazement, as she ran she suddenly found herself lifted high in the air. With each leap, she bounced higher and higher until she was airborne and circling around the schoolhouse, and all the children were looking up at her from the ground below and shouting to her, "Come down! Come down!"

Someone shook Dora's shoulder. She started and looked up. A strange man peered down at her. "Wake up, will you!" the Columbian guard said. "We've been calling and calling to them to come down, but they won't. Is that one yours?" He pointed to Tess in a tree. Wilbur was happily splashing knee-deep in the cool lagoon. His outfit was soaked.

"Wilbur! Tess!" Dora said and scrambled to her feet. She rushed to retrieve her sister, who had cleverly climbed the tree to get away from Wilbur. Dora grabbed Wilbur from the water. "What time is it, sir?" she asked.

"Nearly three forty-five," the guard replied.

Dora gasped. "We're going to be late!"

"And I don't have to say that I don't want you coming around this part of the park again. You've caused me enough problems."

"Sorry, so sorry, sir," Dora said. She grabbed Wilbur by the back of his soggy sailor suit. Now what was she going to do? His mother would be so angry with her. She'd probably assume he'd catch a cold. And it would be Dora's fault. And she wouldn't be paid. "Come over here," she told Wilbur. In desperation, she considered taking off his clothes and wringing them out with her hands, but if his mother found him running naked, she'd be furious. "Dash about!" she told Wilbur as they ran south along the North Canal toward the Great Basin. She knew running was something Wilbur was good at, and perhaps the wind and the hot sun would dry his clothing. Wilbur weaved in and out among sightseers. By the time they reached the elk statue, his clothing was not so soggy.

"Now where are they?" Dora said. She scanned the area for a sign of Ben, his chair, and Mr. and Mrs. Thaw. Fortunately, it wasn't long before they appeared around the corner of the Machinery Building. They were laughing and smiling. Clearly, they had had a wonderful day without their beastly son. Dora greeted them as cheerfully as she could. She handed Mrs. Thaw the basket after she removed Nancy.

"Well, I hope you had a good time, darling," Mrs. Thaw said to Wilbur, who raced around and around the wheeled chair. "What did you learn today?"

Dora held her breath.

"Arms float," Wilbur said. It was the first words he had spoken all day. Dora looked at him in shock.

"Such an intelligent, clever child!" Mr. Thaw said. "And I'm glad to see that he ate his lunch. This is for you." He peeled away a dollar bill from a great roll of money.

Ben smiled at Dora. "She did a good job, didn't she?"

"She certainly did," Mrs. Thaw said. "Would you like to spend some time with Dora tomorrow, Wilbur?"

Dora held her breath again. Wilbur licked his

lips and nodded. Dora didn't know whether to feel glad or terrified.

"We'll see you tomorrow then. Same time, same place. We still have the whole Fine Arts Building to cover," Mr. Thaw said in a businesslike voice. "Right, Ben?"

"Yes, sir," Ben said. "Shall we be going?"

Dora waved weakly. She held the dollar in her fist. "That boy," Tess said as she cradled Nancy, "is so mean."

Dora nodded and sighed. "You're right, Tess. You're absolutely right. Now let's go get our sisters." Together they walked north toward the Children's Building.

Chapter 8

"Good-bye!" Phoebe called that evening to the stout woman who sat at the desk near the entrance to the Children's Building. Dora, Lillian, and Tess waited outside. They planned to walk back to the dormitory together.

"Good-bye, Phoebe dear," the woman called back and scribbled something in her big book.

"Everyone is so nice here," Phoebe said when she rejoined Dora and her sisters. "The ladies are interested in everything. They ask me all kinds of questions and they always listen when I talk."

"Questions?" Dora asked nervously as they trudged along. "What kind of questions?"

"You know," Phoebe said. "About our family.

Where we live. The theater. How come Da doesn't live with us. That kind of thing."

Dora bit her lip. She remembered nosy women from the Methodist Church in Nebraska. Sometimes they came sniffing around the ranch and asked why the girls didn't come to town for Sunday school and why Mama was still in bed and it was past noon. Dora couldn't answer. She didn't like those kinds of questions. Even then she sensed in the proud Christian faces of Mrs. Quimby and Mrs. Dunlap something akin to morbid curiosity and a twinge of cruelty. "You shouldn't tell them anything," Dora warned Phoebe. "You should keep your mouth shut. I saw that woman with the Travelers' Aid Society uniform writing something down. She knows your name. Maybe she keeps a record."

"Maybe she talks to the police," Lillian added, just to make Phoebe squirm.

"The police?" Phoebe exploded. "I haven't done anything wrong."

"You can never be too careful. The fair's crawling with guards and Pinkertons," Lillian said with authority.

"Come on now. I've got a dollar. Let's go to that cheap cafe and have something to eat," Dora said, hoping to change the subject. "You should hear what trouble I went through to earn this money."

But neither of her sisters seemed the least bit interested in hearing about her hard day baby-sitting. They weren't even excited when she told them she could take them out for an inexpensive dinner.

"I ate already," Phoebe boasted. "A real fancy sit-down meal with a white tablecloth and two green vegetables, melt-in-your-mouth biscuits, and fried chicken. Miss Larrabee is a wonderful cook. She fed the Broom Brigade and showed us how to fold napkins and what fork to use. She said all mothers are not fitted to train up infants in the way they should go. She's the kindest, most gener-ous person in the world. Look what she gave me." Phoebe pulled from her pocket a dozen penny postcards with pictures from the fair. She thumbed through them quickly.

Lillian was too busy admiring the Ferris wheel in the distance to pay much attention to the cards. "Will you look at that?" Lillian said. "Now there's some-thing. The most beautiful thing I ever seen." She skipped along beside Dora, Phoebe, and Tess. Lillian's happy face was stained purple around the mouth. "Well, I had something better than fried chicken and postcards happen to me today," Lillian bragged. "I had a picnic with my new friends and we had salami and ice cream and Welch's Grape Drink."

"New friends?" Dora asked suspiciously. "Who are they?"

"Children my own age," Lillian replied. She flashed a sidewise glance at her nosy sister. "One's named James. He and his friends are rich and they're very funny and they're very smart. They know everything."

"Do they work in the Children's Building?" Dora asked.

Lillian sniffed. "Some days."

Dora thought about all the fancy, well-heeled tourists and their children she'd seen around the fair. The Children's Building seemed respectable enough. It attracted the better sort of person. "Is James a nice boy?" Dora asked, careful to stress the word *nice* as if it really meant something else. Something important.

"Very nice," Lillian replied.

"You just be careful," Dora warned. She didn't want her sister associating with a rascal. And yet she felt very helpless. If she told Mama, Mama would just say, "Keep your eye on Lillian." But Dora knew she couldn't keep her eye on her restless sister every minute. She'd just have to hope and pray Lillian had the good sense to stay out of trouble.

For the next several days, the mornings at the dormitory assumed a kind of routine. Every day Dora woke her sisters so that they'd get to work on time. She had to make sure that Phoebe got to the Broom Brigade and Lillian arrived for her sweeping job. Meanwhile, Dora and Tess had to get ready to meet Mr. and Mrs. Thaw so that they could take care of Wilbur. As far as Dora was concerned, the only bright moment in her whole day was seeing Ben.

Mama slept later and later. She was working the lunch and evening shift so she didn't have to wake up so early. She merely groaned when the sun came skimming through the window. Then she rolled over and put a pillow over her head. As days passed, she became grumpier and grumpier. She stopped wearing her fake-cherry hat. She stopped pulling her stockings up or making sure her shoes were clean and shining. It seemed to Dora as if Mama had stopped caring how she looked.

"We're leaving, Mama," Dora called quietly as she opened the door and shoved her sisters out into the hallway. "Can we take a couple nickels for the trolley? We're kind of late today."

"Money's on the table," Mama mumbled.

Dora walked quickly across the room to the coffee can, where Mama kept her fees from the restaurant. Dora was surprised to discover a small crumpled piece of paper jammed under the can. She slipped the paper out and felt instantly happy. Da's handwriting! She knew it anywhere. How many days had gone by since they'd seen him? Seemed like forever. Why hadn't Mama told them that he'd written? She glanced at Mama, who was snoring, and read quickly:

Melba:
Can't come by Sunday as planned. Got to work.
Money scarce. Used up all my paycheck to pay
off some debts with the boys. And of course
the new saddle. Hope the girls are doing fine.
Don't be so sore at me. Will try to get over
maybe next month.

—Earl

Dora reread the note again. Her face felt flushed. Why wasn't he going to see them till next month? That was a very long time. And why was Mama mad at him? What had he done?

"Dora, come on!" Phoebe called. "Miss Larrabee said I can't be late today. We got a big tour of visitors from Wisconsin coming through."

Dora hurriedly jammed the note back under the can, grabbed four nickels, and shut the door softly.

"What's the matter with you?" Lillian demanded. "We been waiting out here forever."

Dora did not say anything. She held Tess's hand as they walked to the cable car. "Awful quiet," Lillian said, turning to inspect Dora. "Cat got your tongue?"

"Nope," Dora said. "Just thinking." She watched the regular group who threw dice against the stoop next to the barbershop. Their dimes and nickels and pennies lay in a glittering pile. The shouting, swearing men were so absorbed that they didn't even look up when the girls carefully walked around them. What had the note said? "... *pay off some debts with the boys.*" Suddenly Dora understood. She knew why Mama was so furious.

Da was gambling again.

Maybe he'd lost all his paycheck. That was what had happened the last time and the time before that. Pretty soon there had been no money left and the man with the top hat from the bank had come and pretty soon they'd been moving out in the night so their neighbors and all the other people they owed money to wouldn't see them.

"Stop squeezing so tight, Dorie," Tess complained and yanked her hand away.

"Sorry," Dora said. She had to keep this quiet from her sisters. They'd only worry.

The girls climbed on the trolley. "I can pay myself," Lillian insisted. She dropped her coin into the grip man's box. Phoebe did the same. They took the seat in front of Dora and sleepy Tess and kept right on talking as if Dora couldn't hear them. "I wish she'd adopt me," Phoebe said matter-of-factly. Dora's ears pricked up, and she leaned forward. "Miss Larrabee's got a genuine Othello range with an extra large oven and solid oak parlor furniture. I know for a fact she has the latest Turkish sofa, rocker, gent's easy chair, and reception chair because she showed us the advertisement."

Lillian scratched her forehead. "I got four dollars and seventy-six cents so far."

"I bet her pretty little house looks just like a Wards Catalog. Absolutely perfect."

"I been on the Ferris wheel already ten times this week. 'Course, the first time was the best. But I still like the way my stomach gets jumpy."

Phoebe shook her head. "I don't know. Looks pretty scary to me."

Dora couldn't help herself. She leaned forward and gripped Lillian firmly by the back of the neck. "What do you mean you went on the Ferris wheel *ten* times?" she hissed in her ear.

Lillian and Phoebe looked over their shoulders at Dora in startled amazement. "Why should you care?" Lillian said angrily and twisted free. "Not your money. Not Mama's neither."

"You know you're not supposed to go on the Ferris wheel alone," Dora said, her eyes squinty with rage. She had not even gone on the Ferris wheel once, and she was twelve. Meanwhile, her eight-year-old sister had been on it ten times in one week. Dora felt humiliated.

"I didn't go alone," Lillian said airily. "I have my own friends who went with me. James promised to buy me some of that Cracker Jack, a bottle of Welch's Grape Drink, and a package of Juicy Fruit gum. He even promised to show me the Streets of Cairo."

"Lucky!" Phoebe murmured. Clearly she was impressed that her sister got to try the latest treats.

"What?" Dora exploded. "Who is James?"

"I told you about him already," Lillian said in a bored voice. "He's *nice*. Now leave me alone."

Dora took a deep breath and leaned back in her seat. She was still fuming with anger and jealousy. *James*. How come Lillian got to do everything fun while she had to take care of whiny Tess and that horrid boy, Wilbur? It wasn't fair. Why, she hadn't even done one fun thing yet at the fair. The whole thing would be over before she got to the Midway Plaisance.

The trolley bumped and ground to a halt. "Sixtieth Street!" the conductor shouted. The girls climbed off and entered the fairgrounds using their passes. Dora did not even need to remind her sisters to carry the pass or how to show it. Phoebe and Lillian marched right through as if they didn't even need Dora anymore to help them do anything. As if they were already grown up. "Don't forget—," Dora began.

"We know, we know," Phoebe said impatiently. "We'll meet you at five o'clock and don't be late." Lillian followed Phoebe into the Children's Building. It wasn't even eight o'clock and already there was a line of parents trying to get their children into the nursery. The admission fee was only twenty-five cents, which paid for fresh milk and a meal. A real bargain.

"Toys! Toys!" Tess said and pointed toward the Children's Building.

"No, Tess," Dora replied. She tugged her youngest sister toward the elk statue, their regular meeting place with Mr. and Mrs. Thaw. "We can't go inside the nursery. We have to watch Wilbur, remember?"

Tess pouted. She hated Wilbur. Dora couldn't blame her. He had tried to bite her twice the day before, and he did not ever want to do anything except run around in circles or torture ducks. He was a dull, beastly child. "And I have a dull, beastly life," Dora decided. She tried hard to smile when she saw Ben trundling up with his rolling chair. His face was red, and he acted as if he didn't see her. Dora frowned.

There wasn't much breeze. Already heat shimmered from the ground. She imagined that up above the ground on the Ferris wheel, the air was probably much cooler, much fresher, much better.

"Good-bye, darling," Mrs. Thaw called to Wilbur after she'd dropped him off and handed Dora the basket with the boring, nutritious picnic. "We're off to the Movable Sidewalk on the Casino Pier. Then we're going to see Columbus's three caravels, the *Niña*, the *Pinta*, and the *Santa Maria*."

Halfheartedly, Dora waved. She watched the rolling chair disappear. As Dora herded Tess and Wilbur north, she kept craning her neck past the Transportation Building and the Horticulture Building toward the Midway Plaisance, which stretched westward directly behind the Women's Building. It was a long, crowded, exotic avenue 600 feet wide and nearly a mile in length. Everything exciting was there—including the Ferris wheel. She had heard there were people in all kinds of outfits playing barbaric music, dancing, doing acrobatic feats and sword fights. She looked down at Wilbur, who had been forbidden by his parents to lay his eyes on such a place. If she tried to sneak him there, he'd certainly tell them and ruin everything. Besides, she didn't want to go there with Wilbur or Tess. They'd only slow her down and complain and fight. She trudged on in a dull, plodding way.

When they reached the Women's Building, Dora considered taking the little bridge to the Wooded Island again. It might be cooler out there among the shady trees. She glanced at the nearby Children's Building and saw that the line of parents and children had disappeared. That was when she made her decision. It was perfect. She'd take Wilbur and Tess to the nursery for fifty cents. They'd have a wonderful time. She'd go to the Midway and come back before Mr. and Mrs. Thaw came back. They'd never see her. They were going to the other side of the fair for the day.

Dora hurried Wilbur and Tess inside the Children's Building to the nursery. Tess was overjoyed. "Toys!" she exclaimed happily. The exhausted nursemaid asked, "Names?" Dora told her, and she scribbled something on the back of two pieces of tan cardboard. She tore these in half.

"Hold still, sonny," she said to wriggling Wilbur as she pinned a number to his back. Then she did the same to Tess. She handed the matching stubs to Dora. "Keep these to reclaim the children at the end of the day. Don't be late. We close at six o'clock." She said something else, but Dora couldn't hear her.

Tess and Wilbur ran off happily. They didn't care one bit that Dora was leaving them with strangers. The great noise of one hundred yelling, screaming, talking, shrieking babies and toddlers was so loud that Dora could hardly hear herself think. She was glad to escape. Quickly, she tucked the tickets in her pocket and dashed around the corner toward the Midway. She was determined to have some fun. She didn't care that she was supposed to be watching the kids.

On the Midway the first thing she saw was the famous Blarney Castle from Ireland. Inside was supposed to be the Blarney Stone, which everyone kissed for good luck. But Dora had heard from Lillian that the stone was actually just a chunk of Chicago sidewalk, so she didn't bother to stop. People stood in a great long line outside the castle. The crowd was just as thick outside the miniature Irish Village, the Japanese Bazaar, and the Hagenbeck Animal Show. There were trained tigers and lions and a thousand parrots. But Dora wasn't interested in these.

Instead, she headed toward the Javanese Village. Dora walked slowly among the eighty thatched, circular huts. The people who lived here had bright brown skin that shone like polished wood. The men's arms and shoulders were decorated with intricate blue designs. They spoke a language Dora did not recognize. Some of them were acrobats, some were jugglers; others did strange dances and played music unlike anything she'd heard before. Their clothes were skimpy, and Dora wondered if they felt embarrassed. The people did not seem to care. They walked about barefoot. Dora wished she could take off her shoes, too.

The natives didn't pay any attention to Dora or the other gawkers as they went about their business of weaving and chatting and pounding something disgusting in a flat wooden platter using a big stick. Dora felt invisible. She wondered if they really lived in the thatched huts all the time. For some reason, she thought of Phoebe as she watched the young girls from Borneo and Samoa and Fiji sweeping the ground with branches. They laughed and chattered just like the girls from Broom Brigade, only there wasn't any tinny piano music in the background and there wasn't any glass window to look through. Dora thought that being a Javanese girl must be more interesting than being a member of the Broom Brigade.

She walked on past the large German village with its moated castle. The smell of beer was very strong, and there was a band that played oom-pah-pah music while people sat around in chairs. Beyond that was the Dahomey village, which also had a series of huts. Peddlers sat outside and sold carved wooden objects with grotesque faces. Other performers demonstrated chilling war cries and chants and swung around shrunken heads and rattling bones. "Cannibals," said a fat tourist in a tight celluloid collar. He was wearing fashionable summer flannels and a flat straw hat called a skimmer.

Dora moved quickly away. She didn't want to be eaten.

Finally, she reached the place she really wanted to see. The noisy, colorful Streets of Cairo thronged with people and animals. The people wore sandals and long white robes and cloth wrapped around their heads. There seemed to be hundreds of Arab men and splendid-looking women. Dogs and donkeys loped past. Some men rode by on enormous shaggy camels, which were decorated with handsome velvet saddles. She was stunned. A camel was much bigger than any horse she had ever seen. She wondered how the rider got up there between the humps. She wondered how he'd get down.

Dora stood very still and felt swallowed up by the strange place—the incomprehensible voices, eerie music, and spicy smells. For the first time, she wished her sisters were there with her. It would be so much better to have someone to share this moment with, she decided.

"Come see the sword dancers!" a serious-faced barker called from outside a theater. "Candle dancers! See the Hootchy-Kootchy dancers!"

Dora turned and watched the crowd, mostly made up of men, file inside. A sign declared, SPLENDID SPECIMENS OF ORIENTAL BEAUTY AND LITTLE EGYPT. There was a picture of a dancing, mysterious woman with a dreamy smile, her painted eyes half-closed, her white teeth showing between very red lips. She was barefoot and she was wearing a flimsy outfit.

"Hey!" someone called.

Dora turned in time to see the blond boy they had seen the first day outside the Children's Building calling for people to come in and see the babies. He was smiling as if he knew her. Over one shoulder he had a sign that said, FRESH LEMONADE 5 CENTS. He was pushing a cart through the crowded bazaar. The cart had a picture of a lemon on it. Every so often he rang the bell. "You're Lill's sister," the boy said. "She told me all about you."

"Who . . . who are you?" Dora stammered. Strangers never called Lillian "Lill."

"I'm James. I'm her friend. Have a lemonade. It's free."

Dora felt her face flush bright red. "You!" she exclaimed with contempt and began to walk away.

"Don't be so uppity. The lemonade is fresh. Really," James persisted. He handed her a cup. Dora paused and licked her lips. She was thirsty. She took a sip. "See? I told you it's good. Just wait here a minute, will you?" In a flash, he ditched the cart behind a snake charmer's exhibit. "So, you look a little bewildered. Maybe you'll let me show you around." He waved to Bedouins who ambled past with baskets in their arms.

"Hi, James!" they called back to him.

"You seem to know a lot of people around here," Dora said suspiciously. She didn't want to talk to him. She knew he was a little con-artist. A scoundrel. A flimflam. But here she was having a conversation. She didn't know why. She just started walking with him. There was something hypnotic about his friendly, open manner.

"Sure. I know everybody," James said, grinning. "Say, I bet you've never been to the Esquimaux Village. Ever seen blubber?"

Dora shook her head. "What's an Esquimaux?"

"Someone who lives far to the north where it's snowy all the time and they make their houses out of ice." James walked faster and faster. They left the Midway and headed directly north, past the buildings representing California, Nebraska, Washington, and North Dakota. Dora wondered if he knew where he was going. When they finally reached the Esquimaux exhibit, they came upon several families sitting outside huts. There were many children and even a small baby among the group. They all wore thick coats with hoods and soft boots. They seemed nearly as miserable as their beautiful gray dogs, who lay in the shade panting. The dogs were attached to what looked like a sled.

As soon as they saw James, they began to smile. "James!" they called to him. They put down their spears and waved for him to come closer. The tourists who were watching looked surprised. Perhaps they had not expected the savage Esquimaux to speak English.

James motioned for Dora to come closer. "Here are my friends," he said. "They've been in Chicago longer than anybody else at the fair."

While Dora stood there, unable to think of anything to say or do, James vanished. The Esquimaux brushed flies from their faces. They had dark eyes that inspected her thoroughly. When James returned he was expertly carrying half a dozen ice cream cones, which he distributed to the eager Esquimaux children. They were delighted and licked the cold, creamy ice cream very rapidly. One of the boys, who looked about Tess's age, pulled off his hood for a moment.

"Put that hood back on!" a loud voice shouted.

The Esquimaux turned and looked impassively at a man in a fancy suit. He had a moustache and a nasty smile. "You know the contract. We've been through all this before. Wear fur clothes or you get no food. Where'd you get that ice cream?"

"I gave it to them, sir," James spoke up, "compliments of Columbia concessions. We sell a lot more ice cream when people see Esquimaux eating it. And what's good for our business is good for your business." He smiled a charming smile. The man wandered away.

"That guy keeps them practically like prisoners," James grumbled to Dora as soon as the man was out of earshot. "Made all kinds of promises to give them pork, bread, molasses, tea and rifles, powder and shot he never kept. So they took him to court."

Dora nodded. For the first time, she felt a begrudging respect for James. She watched the children finishing the ice cream, and she wondered what it would be like to be on display like this all summer long. She watched the crowd peer at the Esquimaux for a few seconds and then wander away. She thought of the Broom Brigade behind glass. That was what the tourists did to her sister, too.

"Dare you to eat an ostrich egg," James said after they said farewell and left the Esquimaux.

Dora made a face.

"Your sister tried one," he said as they returned to the Midway. After hearing that, Dora tried one, too. She was surprised that it tasted like a chicken egg. The thirty big birds were strange-looking creatures with long necks.

The rest of the afternoon she enjoyed a trip to a tea house and a ride in the captive balloon that hovered several hundred feet above the ground, attached by a long safety line. She had never had so much fun. Suddenly, she remembered Wilbur and Tess. "I've got to go," she said. "I'm late. I'm supposed to pick up my sister and a little boy at the Children's Building nursery and get them back to the Columbian Fountain, and I don't even know where I am."

"Don't worry," James said. "I'll get you there in

no time." He put his fingers to his lips and whistled a piercing whistle. Instantly, one of the rolling chair pushers appeared. He doffed his cap to James. "Take her to the Children's Building, pronto."

The chair pusher trotted faster than the wind. He seemed to know how to dodge the crowds as he careened down empty back ways and side streets. Breathlessly, he stopped in front of the Children's Building. "What do I pay you?" she asked anxiously. She had only a nickel.

"Nothing," the chair pusher said. "You're a friend of James."

Dora dashed inside and ran up the steps to the nursery. Most of the babies were gone. Poor Tess sat in the middle of the room crying and crying. Wilbur was nowhere to be seen. She reached in her pocket to give the nursemaid the tickets. They were gone! She thought they must have fallen out of her pocket on the balloon ride. Now she was going to be in terrible trouble.

"I'm afraid we can't release the children without proper identification," the nursemaid said.

Dora groaned. "You have to. That's my sister, Tess, right over there." Tess ran to Dora as soon as she saw her.

"What is the other child's name?" the woman said wearily.

"Wilbur," Dora replied.

The woman made a gasping noise. "You can take that boy with you as soon as you can. Little monster. And don't ever bring him back here again." The woman corralled Wilbur, who was rocking on a hobbyhorse back and forth over a doll's head. The nursemaid pointed them both toward the door.

Dora took each child by the hand and dashed toward the elk statue. "Sorry I'm late," she said in a breathless voice to Mr. and Mrs. Thaw, who were sitting on a bench and looking very angry. "Time just slipped away."

"Young lady," Mr. Thaw said, "we could have gone to two more exhibits while we were sitting around waiting for you to appear. You're fired." He handed her a dollar, loaded up his wife and child in the chair, and pointed to Ben to begin pushing. Ben did not even look at Dora.

Dora didn't care. For once, she had had a wonderful time. "Good-bye!" she called softly. She watched them trundle away. Wilbur scrambled out of his mother's lap and loped along beside the rolling chair. That was when Dora noticed the cardboard nursery number that was still pinned to his back.

Chapter

9

As Dora and Tess walked back to meet Phoebe and Lillian, Dora read aloud the words carved over one of the doors to the Children's Building: "Just as the twig is bent the tree's inclined." She had never understood what that meant until now. Whatever happened to a young tree would affect it when it grew older. Suddenly, Dora felt awful. She had probably ruined Tess forever by leaving her at the nursery and making her think her sister wasn't ever coming back, that she'd been abandoned.

"I am so sorry, Tess." Dora paused to wipe her sister's sticky, tear-stained face. "I didn't mean to forget you. It's just that time seemed to get away. And I—"

"We had crackers with milk," Tess said. She looked up at the roof of the Children's Building.

Along the roof's edge, nets had been set up. "I ate bologna for lunch. Wilbur threw his down."

"From the roof?"

Tess nodded. "He poked the pretty doll's eyes out."

Dora rubbed the back of her neck. She was glad she wasn't going to have to take care of Wilbur again. She decided she would turn over a new leaf, just like Da had said. Running away to the Midway had been wrong. From now on, she vowed, she would try and do a better job of taking care of Tess and keeping her sisters together.

When Phoebe and Lillian emerged from the Children's Building, they each were carrying a sack. "What's that?" Tess demanded.

"Surprise," Phoebe said mysteriously. "Lillian knows a great place. Come on!"

Dora wondered where they were going. Was it some secret hideout Lillian had learned from James? Instead of being her usual bossy self, Dora didn't ask any questions or give any orders. She simply followed Phoebe and Lillian. They hurried inside the Manufactures Building. Inside they took a terrifying, 220-foot-tall elevator.

"Look!" Lillian said, giggling.

The girls followed her out onto the roof and discovered a breathless view of the fair. Everything seemed so far away. The buildings, the people—all looked like toys. They could see for miles. "Amazing!" Dora whispered.

"Come over here where there's a nice breeze," Lillian said. She placed the bag on the ground, and they all sat down.

"Here you go," Phoebe said proudly. She took out corn bread and veal cutlets and great slabs of apple pie. Everything was wrapped in clean newspaper. "I made these today in the Corn Kitchen. We'll have a picnic—just like the other tourists."

Dora stopped Tess before she dug into the apple pie with her dirty fingers. "What about a fork or spoon?"

"Forgot those," Phoebe said. "Sorry."

"I've got some," Lillian said in a helpful voice. "I may not be able to cook, but I'm good at winning prizes. Here are some souvenir spoons." She took from her pocket a fistful of spoons decorated with Liberty Bells. Each girl took one and began eating eagerly.

"Delicious!" Dora said with her mouth full.

Little by little, the sky turned red, then purple as the sun set. A cool lake breeze ruffled the newspapers. "Wish Da were here," Lillian said quietly. "Mama, too."

Nobody spoke. Dora thought about the note

that she'd found that morning, and she felt a hollow, bitter feeling in her throat. She didn't want to ruin the lovely picnic — the first time all four of them had done anything enjoyable together in a very long time. She didn't say anything.

Phoebe carefully rolled up the newspapers and stuffed them in the sack. "The show's not over yet," Lillian said. She stood up and motioned to the edge of the observation area. Stars twinkled. The other people on the top of the building seemed hushed.

"Maybe we should go home now," Dora said. She knew Mama would be worried.

"Not yet!" Lillian said. "Just a few more minutes. You'll never see anything like this again."

And in a surprising flash, thousands of white lights illuminated the buildings. Lights outlined the Ferris wheel spokes. Lights reflected on the water. "Fairyland, isn't it?" Phoebe said.

Dora nodded. The crowd on the roof applauded. The girls clapped and cheered, too. "Come on," Lillian said. "Follow me."

"Where are we going now?" Phoebe demanded.

"The Ferris wheel," Lillian replied. "I've been on it twenty-three times. And you haven't tried it. Come on. I know the operator. He's a friend."

Dora took Tess and followed her sisters back

down the elevator to the first floor of the Manufactures Building. They hurried across the mysterious Wooded Island, past the Women's Building, to the Midway. For once, no one was waiting in line for the Ferris wheel. Nervously, Dora and Phoebe clambered after Lillian, who held up Tess for the Ferris wheel operator to see. He nodded and smiled at her and waved them through.

"Come on!" Lillian called to her sisters.

Dora looked up through the giant spiderweb of girders decorated with white lights. The Ferris wheel seemed impossibly tall, impossibly fragile. She gulped. The girls climbed through the door of one of the thirty-six cars made of wood and iron and paneled with plate glass windows. Gingerly, Dora took a seat in one of the forty swivel chairs inside. Her hands were sweating. She felt as if she was going to be sick. The door slammed shut.

Phoebe gave a little scream. Tess clapped her hands together. "Up! Up!" she shouted.

"Two hundred fifty feet," Lillian said. "That's how high we're going." The car jerked and suddenly lifted off the ground a few feet, stopped, and began to rock a little.

Dora gripped the arms of the chair. "What's happening?"

"The Ferris wheel has to stop to let more people on," Lillian said with authority. "We'll be stopping about twelve times on the whole trip. Don't worry, we'll start going again soon."

Phoebe looked pale. She tried to keep her eyes on the darkening horizon. Lillian, who had been on the Ferris wheel countless times, wasn't a bit afraid. "Here we go!" she called gaily. Dora's stomach lurched. They rose slowly into the air, higher and higher.

"Up we're going on the Ferris wheel!" Lillian sang out. "Down we're going. How does it feel?" Tess clapped happily. In spite of her initial terror, Dora was enchanted by the sight of the fair and the Midway below. She felt as if she were flying above some kind of fairy kingdom. Could Da see them up here? she wondered. They climbed higher and higher on the Ferris wheel, nearly to the top. That was when Dora felt as if all the breath was knocked out of her. She couldn't speak. She had this terrible feeling that they would be catapulted off into space. But at the last minute, the car began a gentle descent.

"Down!" Tess cried happily.

They made two revolutions. And then the ride was over. Someone swung open the door. They stood up and climbed unsteadily down from the platform to solid ground. Dora's knees buckled a little, but she laughed. "Wonderful!" she whispered.

"I wasn't scared a bit," Phoebe lied.

"Go again!" Tess screamed

"Not now. Maybe another time," Lillian said. Her face was glowing. She'd enjoyed sharing the ride with her sisters.

"We'd better go home. It's late," Dora said. The girls headed home on the trolley. They tried to be very quiet as they tiptoed up the stairs to their room. But when they opened the door, they could tell that Mama wasn't there. Her bed was empty. Phoebe lit a candle and shut the door.

"Where is she?" Lillian said in a worried voice.

"Still at work," Dora replied. She hoped her voice sounded calm. Her heart pounded angrily. "All right, let's get ready for bed."

The girls quietly got into their beds. It was nearly ten-thirty. Dora frowned. Other mothers would have been waiting for them. They would be angry and yell for disobeying. Why couldn't Mama be like other mothers? Didn't she care about them? Dora punched her pillow. "Good night," she said to her sisters.

Late that night in the dark, there was a thump and a rattle. The door squeaked open. "Mama?" Phoebe whispered, wide-awake. She hoped it wasn't a burglar.

"Shshshsh!" Mama said angrily. She knocked over something in the dark. There was a dull thud. "Ow!" She swore and kicked a piece of furniture.

Dora held her breath, listening to the angry noises. She hoped Mama would not wake up her sisters. No such luck.

"Mama!" Lillian said in a sleepy voice. "We went on the Ferris wheel."

Mama sat down on the edge of the bed to pull off her shoes. She threw each one down loudly on the floor. Even though Dora could not see her face, she knew that Mama was angry.

"Mama, we had a picnic," Lillian whispered.

"Glad someone's enjoying themselves," Mama said bitterly.

Dora took a deep breath. It wasn't fair to ruin their good time just because she'd had a bad day at work.

"Mama, get me water!" Tess whined.

Mama made an exhausted noise with her breath. "Dora, can you get it for her? I'm beat."

Dora moved across the room carefully, trying not to knock into the edge of the bed. She could hear someone talking below them. Any moment Miss Starkweather was going to start knocking on their door complaining about the noise again. Why didn't Mama ever seem to care about disturbing their neighbors?

"Shut up!" Mama said in a low voice to the voices beneath them. She stamped her foot on the thin boards.

"Mama!" Dora hissed. "You don't need to do that. You'll only make it worse. What if they throw us out?"

"Don't care. Can't get any worse than it is."

"What do you mean?" Dora said. There was something chilling in Mama's words.

"I mean I got fired," she said and snorted. "I don't care. It was an awful job. Clearly beneath me."

Dora felt stunned. So did her sisters. "Fired?" Lillian said in disbelief.

"How will we pay the rent?" Phoebe asked in a quavering voice.

"I need to find a job that suits me," Mama said. She moved around the room and knocked into furniture. "I need to get back on stage. I can't sling any more hash for anybody. I'm an actress. I'm talented. Don't you forget it."

The girls sat silently. Fear filled the room. "Mama," Dora said in as calm a voice as she could muster, "we need that money. There aren't any jobs over at the Wild West Show. Buffalo Bill told us. What you did was irresponsible."

Mama laughed unpleasantly. "I'll tell you about irresponsible. Your father. Now there's the irresponsible one."

"Da?" Lillian said.

Dora knew exactly what Mama was going to say. She waited, filled with dread.

"He's no help. Leaving me over here to slave away while he has a good old time with that sporting crowd. And he promised. He told me he wouldn't. I was a fool to believe him. I was a fool to let him out of my sight."

"Can't you ask him for money?" Phoebe asked nervously.

"There is no money," Mama said in a sullen voice. "It's gone. He spent it on horse races or poker. I don't know what."

Phoebe began to cry. Lillian put her hand on her sister's trembling shoulder. Then Tess started crying. She didn't know why, she just started crying because Phoebe was.

"Mama, you've got to get a different job," Phoebe said and wiped her face with the bedsheet. "You've got to find something."

"Don't worry, girls," Mama said. She threw back the covers and climbed into bed. "I have a new plan. A better plan. Everything's under control. Tomorrow I have an audition."

"Wonderful!" Lillian exclaimed. "Where?"

"Streets of Cairo," she said proudly and pulled the trunk from under her bed.

Phoebe stopped whimpering. "What?" she demanded in horror.

"You can't be a hootchy-kootchy dancer," Dora said. "It's not proper."

"Why not?" Lillian said. "Mama's a good dancer."

"That's right, Lillian," Mama said. Her voice sounded brighter.

"You can't because you're not an Arab," Dora said slowly, as if her mother were a very small child. "Little Egypt is foreign. You are from Kansas."

"So?" Mama said in a petulant voice. She opened the hatbox and pulled out the purple sequined costume that she wore in *The Count of Monte Cristo.* The fabric rustled. "All I need is a black wig. I can learn any dance. I can dance with the best of them. I'm a professional actress, don't you ever forget it." She stood up and made a belly-dance movement. "I bet those girls are fakes anyhow. I'll show them. You just wait."

Lillian laughed and clapped. Phoebe hid her eyes. "What will the girls say? What will Miss Larrabee think of me now?" Phoebe said and moaned. "My mother—a hootchy-kootchy girl. It's unseemly."

"I think it's wonderful," Lillian said. "Good luck. That's all I have to say."

Wearily, Dora picked up Tess and put her back in bed. She blew out the candle. She'd had enough of her mother's high-flown fantasies and irresponsible promises for one night. Deep down, she knew what was really going to happen tomorrow. She was going to have to go to the fair with Tess bright and early and look for another paying job. Somewhere, anywhere. Both she and her mother had been fired on the same day. But Dora knew that she had a better chance of finding a new job than her mother did of finding a position as a dancer.

Dora climbed into bed and rolled over. She was glad no one could see her angry face. She had hoped to save some of the money she'd made so that maybe one day she could go back to school. Now there was no chance for that. Any money she or her sisters made was going to have to be used to help pay the rent and buy food.

Chapter

10

The next morning Dora and her sisters crept out of their beds as noiselessly as possible. It was as if the argument and bitter feelings from the night before had lingered in the room like the smell of cooked cabbage or stale cigar smoke. "Hurry up, now," Dora said irritably to Lillian and Phoebe. She did not want to wake their mother, who was still snoring. She did not want to talk to their mother.

"Nancy, poor, poor Nancy," Tess murmured. She cradled her armless doll and rocked her back and forth.

"We don't have any time to deal with Nancy right now," Lillian said as she slipped her shoes on. "You have to leave her here."

"Her arm!" Tess said, the pitch of her voice rising to a dangerously piercing level. "You promised, Dorie. You promised to fix her." She held out Nancy's battered, severed arm, now muddy and bent. The stuffing was coming out one end.

"We have no needle or thread," Dora whispered.

Tess's bottom lip stuck out and began to quiver. Any minute she was about to launch into a full-blown fit.

"Look," Dora said desperately, "when we get home today after work, I'll borrow a needle and thread from the lady downstairs and I'll fix Nancy. We haven't time now. All right?"

Tess looked suspiciously at her oldest sister. "Promise?"

Dora nodded. She quickly opened the door and motioned for her sisters to follow. The girls were unusually silent on the trolley ride to the fair. They passed a group of people in battered clothes waiting silently, patiently, outside a church. "What's that line about?" Phoebe asked. "It isn't Sunday, is it?"

Dora craned her neck for a better look. There were women, children, and men. Some carried bundles. A few had old syrup pails. "Maybe they're giving something away," she said.

"You bet," the man sitting next to her said. He was dressed in a dark flannel suit and wore an expensive derby. "Food. They're giving away all kinds of canned goods. Those people are out of work. Can't find a job. So they get food." He snorted as if it were the fault of the people in line that they were unemployed.

Dora fidgeted. She scooted as far away from the man in the derby hat as she could for fear he'd start to criticize her next. Seeing those people standing there in line made Dora feel even more desperate. She had to find a job. There had to be something she could do. Luckily, they were at the fair early enough that there were no lines yet.

The girls walked quickly to the Children's Building. The sun was shining, and there was a pleasant, balmy, early morning breeze blowing in from the lake, but none of the girls seemed to notice. "Do you think it's true what Mama said about Da?" Phoebe said in a small voice.

Lillian shrugged. "Maybe we should go over to the Wild West Show and visit Da and make sure he's all right."

"You remember what Buffalo Bill said," Phoebe reminded her. "No girls allowed. If he sees us, Da might get fired, too. Then both our parents will be out of work."

"Maybe we should try and send Da a message," Lillian suggested. "Maybe we should let him know that she lost her job."

Phoebe frowned. "Mama will be furious if she finds out. You know how proud she is."

"We'll wait till tonight. We'll see how her audition goes," Dora said. She walked into the building and said good-bye to Phoebe and Lillian. "Now, Tess, you're the lucky one. You get to go to the nursery while I see if I can get a job in the Roof Garden Cafe in the Women's Building."

Tess let out a wail. "I don't want to go to the nursery. You said I didn't have to go back."

"Can't be helped," Dora said. She tried to sound cheerful. "You'll have fun today, Tess. Wilbur isn't going to be there." She pulled a quarter from her pocket and took a deep breath. At least Tess would get a good meal out of this. At least she'd be safe. Dora took a number and was careful to tuck the stub inside her shoe, where it wouldn't be lost. Tess toddled off happily as soon as she saw their neighbor, Miss Shattuck.

Dora tried to feel confident as she trudged up the steps to the Roof Garden Cafe. She was there early, before the restaurant had officially opened. "Hello," she said to a man in a white shirt who stood near the door. "I'm looking for work. I'll do anything. Wash dishes, clear plates. Anything."

The man carried an armload of large cans of vegetables. "You don't look too big," the man said gruffly. "It's a long day here. We serve hundreds of customers."

"I'm very strong," Dora promised. "I can do the work."

"Just so happens I lost my dishwasher yesterday. Maybe stand on a box, then you can reach?"

Dora smiled eagerly. "Oh, yes. I can wash dishes." She was glad he didn't bother to ask her name. She didn't want him to know who her mother was—the woman who had been fired the day before.

The man hired Dora for half the wages he regularly gave his last dishwasher. That was because Dora was only twelve, he said. A grown man would have made more. Dora didn't care that she was being underpaid. Something was better than nothing. She followed the man into the noisy, hot kitchen. He showed her the three giant tubs sitting on a long table. "You have to fill these with hot water and suds and stack the dishes over here," he said. "You got to move fast. You break any, you pay. Understand?"

Dora nodded. She looked nervously at the great mound of dirty, greasy plates left over from the day before. Cold, scummy water from the day before filled the tubs. Flies buzzed around the congealed food. But she rolled up her sleeves. "What do I have to do with the old water?"

"Dump it in the sink over there," he said, pointing across the slippery floor to the kitchen's only drain. He left.

Dora knew she couldn't carry the tubs across the room to dump them. She found an old bucket and had to carry the water back and forth until she drained it. Then she turned on a faucet and filled the tubs. "Hurry up!" the cook shouted. "We need some plates."

Dora worked quickly. She dipped the dirty plates in the soapy tub and scrubbed them with a rag. Then she dunked them in the clear water and set them on a huge rack. But there always seemed to be more dirty plates, more and more plates. When the customers began arriving, the work became even more grueling.

"Dishes!" the waiters shouted. "We need dishes!"

Dora bent over and worked all morning without stopping. Her hands turned red, and her fingertips wrinkled. Her arms stung from the soap. Her back ached. With every passing minute, the kitchen became hotter and hotter. The cook with the bellowing voice slammed pots and pans. He flung fried, sizzling meats against the stove. He hacked with a sharp blade. His angry face streamed with sweat. "Faster!" he screamed at her. "We need more plates!"

The waiters rushed in and out of the kitchen shouting orders, whisking away more plates, bringing back filthy ones. Dora felt as if she might collapse. Was this how Mama felt?

By mid-afternoon, there was a lull. The cook stomped over to the window and stood smoking a cigarette. He flipped the ashes on the floor. "How old you?" he demanded of Dora.

She told him. The man shook his head. "You a hard worker for such a little girl," he said.

Dora felt faint. She had not eaten anything all day. The cook flipped his cigarette out the window. He took up his huge cleaver and cut away a thick piece of beef and flung it between two thick pieces of bread. He handed this to her with a mug of coffee. "Eat," he said and thudded back behind the stove again.

Dora sat on a crate and ate as fast as she could. She could hear chairs scraping in the dining room. Soon more dirty plates would be arriving again.

All day was the same. When it was nearly five o'clock, Dora got to go home. She collected her fifty cents for her day's work and staggered down the steps to retrieve her sister from the nursery. Dora had never felt so tired in her life. She was glad to see Phoebe and Lillian waiting for them outside the Children's Building. Luckily, Phoebe had worked in the Corn Kitchen again and had brought something for Dora to eat.

"Nancy," Tess said and pulled on Dora's sleeve on the way home on the trolley. "Nancy's arm."

Dora didn't hear her sister. She had fallen asleep. "Come on," Lillian said, shaking Dora by the shoulder. "Let's go see what happened with Mama's audition."

They got off the trolley and went into the dormitory. To their amazement, when they opened the door of their room, a head sat on the table. A head with a black wig—but no Mama. "Do you suppose this is Mama's?" Phoebe asked. She made a horrified face.

Lillian clapped. "She got the job. She's a hootchy-kootchy dancer." She picked up the stiff black wig and placed it on her head and danced around the room. Dora and Tess laughed and laughed, but Phoebe did not think Lillian was funny.

"I have never been so embarrassed in my life," she said, blushing bright red. "If anyone from the Broom Brigade finds out my mother is dancing with Little Egypt, I will die. I will simply die."

That evening Mama still did not come home. Dora went downstairs on a mission. "You watch Tess," she told Phoebe.

Dora crept along the stairway to the woman who sat at the desk near the entrance. "I was wondering, ma'am," Dora said politely to Miss Starkweather, "if I could borrow a needle and thread."

"Needle and thread?" Miss Starkweather demanded. She leaned closer to peer into Dora's face. "Who are you?"

"Dora Pomeroy. I live upstairs in Room 203."

"Oh, I know. You're the loud ones. The noisy girls."

Dora bit her lip. "I have to fix Nancy's arm. I'll bring the needle and thread right back."

"Nancy one of your sisters?"

"Nancy's my sister's doll. She's terribly attached to her."

Miss Starkweather arched one eyebrow. "Where's your mother? Why can't she fix the doll?"

"She's working," Dora replied in a little voice.

Miss Starkweather made a loud harumph, as if this was rather improper. Four young girls left alone. She efficiently snapped open a box from a desk drawer. "Here's the needle and thread. Bring them back. Try to keep the noise level down. We've had enough complaints already. And tell your mother this is her last extension. Rent's due, and this time no excuses. Think you can remember all that?"

Dora nodded nervously. She hoped that the ladies who ran the dormitory didn't know about Mama's new job. Her hands felt very cold as she picked up the needle and thread. And what about the rent? She licked her lips. "I was wondering if I could ask for another favor, ma'am," Dora said softly. "I was wondering if I could send a note over to the Wild West Show."

"Wild West Show? That seems highly improper."

"My father works there. I want to get in touch with him."

"One of *those*, is he? I see. Well, if you want to send a message, I suggest that you use the postal box on the corner. Send a letter that way."

Dora thanked Miss Starkweather and trudged upstairs with the needle and thread. After she finished sewing Nancy's arm back on, she hastily scribbled a note on one of the postcards Phoebe lent her:

Dear Da;
Can you come and see us?
Rent is due. We're short cash.
Hurry. Love, Dora

Dora wrote secretly. She didn't want her sisters to tell Mama what she'd done, so she hurried outside with the postcard that evening. She dropped it in the letter box on Stony Island Avenue with a penny stamp she borrowed from Phoebe.

When she went back to their room, Mama still had not returned. "Come on," Dora said to her sisters. "Time for bed."

That evening, very late, Mama came stumbling into the room. She lit a candle. She was so happy, so noisy, that she woke them all up right away. "I was at a rehearsal. I can't tell you how wonderful it was to be back on stage again. How do you like my outfit?" She twirled around, holding up a filmy pink dancing skirt. Someone knocked below and hollered.

"Shut up yourself!" Mama called. "Isn't it wonderful? The money's not good. Slave wages, really. But it's work. The kind I love best." Her face glowed with a kind of happiness they had not seen in a long time.

"That's wonderful, Mama," Lillian said.

"You are beautiful," Tess added.

Mama smiled and sang softly:

Then come sit by my side if you love me;
Do not hasten to bid me adieu.
But remember the Red River Valley
and the cowboy that loved you so true . . .

Phoebe did not say anything. For a long time, neither did Dora. "Mama?" Dora said finally. "Miss Starkweather says—"

"Who cares what she thinks?" Mama said gaily. "She'll get used to the idea."

"No, Mama," Dora said. She spoke slowly. "She wanted me to tell you that this is the last extension. The rent is due."

Mama did not stop smiling. "You always worry far too much, Dora. Everything's fine. I have a job."

"Yes, but Mama—"

"Yes, but nothing. Now I want you all to come and see the show, of course."

Phoebe frowned. "I don't really think that's proper."

"I'll go," Lillian said enthusiastically. "I'd love to see you perform."

Dora sighed. She could see she wasn't getting anywhere. Not with Mama floating five feet off the ground about being in the theatre again. Mama went deaf sometimes when there was some unpleasantness like rent to think about. "Good night, Mama," Dora said wearily. "I've got to work tomorrow."

"Work, where?" Mama asked. She made strange hand motions and kicked and twirled. Someone knocked from the floor below.

"I'm dishwashing," Dora said quickly. "Look, if you keep dancing around, we're going to get thrown out of here. That woman warned me."

"All right, all right," Mama said and flounced on the bed. "You're no fun, Dora, did you know that?"

Another time, another day, Dora might have laughed. She might have smiled. But somehow Mama's comment did not seem the least bit funny. That night before she went to sleep, Dora prayed that Da would get her postcard.

Days passed. Dora went to work in the restaurant. Tess spent time in the nursery. Phoebe and Lillian went regularly to the Children's Building. And still there was no message from Da. He sent no word, no money. Dora was beginning to feel desperate. Meanwhile, Mama blossomed. She loved the performance, the cheering audience, the notoriety. Everyone knew about Little Egypt—the most popular event at the fair, she liked to remind them.

"Have you heard from Da? Have you told him about your new job?" Dora asked one day.

But Mama only laughed. She sounded bitter and amused at the same time. "No, I haven't heard from him. And no, he doesn't know about my dancing. And I don't care."

Dora knew she was lying. It was part of the little petulant role Mama liked to play, as if she were still on stage. The flirty little ingenue. It drove Dora mad. Mama's schedule meant that she was gone most of the time the girls were home. They saw less and less of her. She worked at night. They worked during the day.

"We see that wig on the stand more than we see Mama," Phoebe complained one afternoon. She was busy writing a postcard to Florence. It said:

Deer Florence:
Went to Fisheries and playd
nickel in slot macheen that
gives EXACT weyt, plays tune
and gives souveneer card and
tells fortune. Heres mine—
For you I see heroic effort
and handsome reward.

— Phoebe

"At least she's happy," Lillian said. She sat on the ground and spread out her collection of World's Columbian Exposition spoons, sashes, ribbons, chromolith cards, glass pen handles, horseshoe pins, a fragrant sandalwood fan, and Columbus scarf.

"Where'd you get all that stuff?" Dora demanded. She dipped her hand in some of Mama's cold cream for removing her heavy hootchy-kootchy makeup. Dora rubbed the thick white cream on her hands and arms, but she could not sooth the chapped, raw skin that was cracking and bleeding in places. "I'm sure you didn't find it on the floor of the gymnasium when you were cleaning up."

Lillian laughed. Dora did not like the harsh sound. "Friends gave me these," Lillian said.

"You mean James?" Dora asked suspiciously. She had not seen him since her afternoon at the Midway.

"James and others," Lillian said.

"Lucky!" Phoebe said. "I wish I had a wonderful postcard collection. I'd take it everywhere with me."

"You can't just carry valuables around with you at the fair. Things get swiped."

"Swiped?" Phoebe asked.

"Let me show you," Lillian said. "Picking somebody's pockets is easy. Look. Put something valuable in your pocket."

Phoebe put her precious Broom Brigade pin in her pocket and walked around the room. She turned away, arms crossed over her chest. Lillian rushed past her. "Now check your pocket," Lillian said.

"Gone!" Phoebe said, horrified. "How'd you do that?"

"Easy. Just takes practice," Lillian replied.

Dora watched this scene with a sense of rising horror. What was happening to her sister? "You know you can go to jail for picking pockets. The Columbian guards are watching all the time," Dora warned.

"I'm not a pickpocket," Lillian said and sniffed. "Don't worry."

But Dora couldn't help herself. She *was* worried. She became even more upset when, one day, while waiting for Phoebe and Lillian she overheard the woman at the desk in the Children's Building say in a low, consoling tone to Phoebe, "Phoebe, dear. I'm so sorry to hear about your mother."

Dora acted like she was tying her boot lace. She leaned closer. She couldn't hear what her sister was murmuring with her sad face. The woman patted Phoebe's arm. Phoebe looked startled when she saw Dora watching her.

"What did you tell her?" Dora said in a low voice as they walked to the trolley.

"I told her our mother had died," Phoebe said simply.

"Died? How could you say something so awful?"

"She might as well be dead," Phoebe replied in a steely voice.

Every day Dora checked the dormitory desk to see if there was a note from Da. Every day she was disappointed. Mama managed to pay part of the rent. She still owed money, but at least Dora did not have to sneak her sisters through the doorway when Miss Starkweather wasn't looking.

In late September, after nearly three months on the job, Dora went to pick up Tess from the nursery the way she did every day. She was surprised to discover Miss Shattuck on duty later than usual. In her arms she was holding a baby boy. His brown hair stuck straight up, and he looked perfectly happy.

"Sorry I'm late," Dora apologized, handing over the cardboard number and retrieving Tess from the "pond," a low, carpeted area with a wall around it that was used as a play area. "Who's that?"

"His name's Charley. That's all we know. He's been here since yesterday," Miss Shattuck said wearily. She handed the little boy to Dora. "I'm exhausted. Stayed here all last night."

"You mean, his parents never showed up?" Dora asked.

Miss Shattuck nodded. "I've never heard of anything so irresponsible. We have the ticket stub.

And I can barely make out the name. There's so many babies here all the time—nearly one hundred fifty some days. I can't keep track of all the mothers." She sat down in a rocking chair. She looked very worried.

Charley grabbed a handful of Dora's hair and gave a hard yank. "What are you going to do?" She couldn't help but think of her own situation. At least Mama had not abandoned them. At least they were old enough to try and figure things out on their own.

"I don't know. Maybe call the police. We'll have to try and find the parents."

For the next several days Dora and her sisters came to the nursery and took turns playing with Charley. They lavished him with attention. Lillian gave him a World's Columbian Exposition rattle, and Phoebe brought him little crackers she baked. Even Tess seemed to enjoy his company. Lillian suggested that it would be nice to have a brother and perhaps they should ask their mother. Naturally, Dora thought this was a very bad idea. She knew who would end up taking care of the new brother.

The girls worried and fretted over Charley. They wondered how long he would be able to live in the nursery, even though the nursemaids had pledged to volunteer their time in regular shifts to take care of him around the clock. Dora and her sisters watched with fascination as the newspapermen arrived at the nursery to interview people.

"Reckless Parents Abandon Baby!" the headlines read. Dora and her sisters couldn't help feeling rather famous themselves. After all, they personally knew Charley. The nursery became even more crowded, noisy, and chaotic as the crowds picked up at the fair. More and more people came to look into the nursery window and see the famous Charley.

And still no mother or father came forward to claim Charley.

As the month of September rolled by, more and more people came to the fair. The restaurant was packed. Dora wondered how much longer she could stand the work. She was beginning to feel as stiff as an old woman. After hours at the washtub, she could bend over only with great effort.

One unseasonably hot late afternoon, Dora went to pick up Tess after a particularly long day in the kitchen. She waited patiently in line, listening to the crying and the hollering. Finally, when it was her turn to claim her sister, she handed one of the new nursemaids her half of the ticket. "Where's Miss Shattuck?" Dora asked.

"Took a vacation," the nursemaid replied. She looked in the wooden box where they kept the stubs. "Sorry, she's gone."

"I know, ma'am," Dora said impatiently. "You told me already. I'm in kind of a hurry. Where's my sister?"

"Gone. That's what I said."

Dora was speechless. "Gone?"

"She's not here. Someone else must have picked her up. Maybe someone else in your family? Next in line, please."

Dora gasped. "Nobody but me ever picks up Tess." She ran out the door and hurried to the place where she was to meet Lillian and Phoebe. They were already standing under a tree, just the two of them.

Dora was breathless. "Did you pick up Tess?"

"Not us," Phoebe replied.

"That's your job," Lillian said.

Dora tried to feel hopeful. "Do you think Mama came?"

"She's at work. Hey, Dora, what's going on?" Phoebe demanded. Now her face was pale, too.

"What happened to Tess?" Lillian demanded.

"She's disappeared," Dora said. She ran into the nursery with her two sisters on her heels. Desperately, they searched the crowd of unclaimed children again. Dora felt as if she were having a terrible nightmare. Any moment she'd wake up. Any moment.

Chapter 11

"Where is your mother?" the nursemaid named Miss Rue asked Dora, when she returned the second time to look for Tess. Behind Dora stood Phoebe and Lillian.

"The Streets of Cairo," Dora mumbled.

Miss Rue had unruly dark eyebrows that jumped when she spoke. "She's visiting?"

"She dances there," Lillian announced, "with Little Egypt."

Phoebe cringed. Miss Rue gasped. "Perhaps we should call the police."

"Why?" Dora asked in a nervous voice. Would they arrest Mama?

"The police can help us search," Miss Rue said. "In the meantime I think I'll contact the Children's

Aid Society." She glanced at Dora. "What does your sister look like?"

Instantly, Dora felt suspicious. She knew that tone of voice, that look. She had heard and seen all this before when the minister's wife back in Seattle had tried to suggest that their mother was unfit. The same look, the same sound that Miss Starkweather had made at the dormitory. "No, no. We don't need the Children's Aid Society," Dora stammered, dreading what these women might do when they found out the girls' mother was a hootchy-kootchy dancer and they had not seen their father since the beginning of the summer.

Dora and her sisters described Tess in detail. Four years old, dark hair, dark eyes. Dirty face. Bad temper. Stubborn. Very strong. Really, it was hard for Dora to imagine someone wanting to kidnap Tess.

"Dora, I don't understand. Why don't they know where Tess is?" Phoebe whined as if Miss Rue wasn't right there, standing in front of them.

"Where is our sister?" Lillian demanded. She glared directly at the nursemaid. "If you lost her, you are going to be in big trouble."

"Nobody lost your sister," Miss Rue muttered. Her hands were trembling as she thumbed once again through that day's receipts. "I cannot believe we are involved in yet another mishap. What will Mrs. Palmer say? First Charley, now this." She pulled something from the box. "Here is the stub. It says her name and the time of departure: 4:30 P.M. But who picked her up? Who?"

"If you call the police, the newspapers will find out right away," Dora said in a low voice. "They'll write about you, but they won't make you a heroine."

Miss Rue's eyebrows danced. She pursed her thin lips together as if she were thinking.

"Give us an hour," Dora begged. "She's only been gone a little while. Let me and my sisters try and find her. Maybe whoever picked her up is still at the fair. Maybe it was a mistake. Another babysitter." Dora thought of her escapade leaving Wilbur. Maybe someone else just like her went back for their employer's child and got mixed up. Dora had to hope this was true. "Don't leave until we return," she made Miss Rue promise. "Stay right here. And if we can't find her, we'll call in the police, the Columbian Guards, the Pinkertons — whoever you want." Miss Rue nodded.

"Let's go," Dora said to her sisters. "Tell anyone who helps to bring Tess back to the Children's Building the moment she's found."

The girls rushed out of the Children's Building at top speed. The girls decided to each take different directions. Phoebe headed for the Wooded Island and the North Pond; Lillian, for the Midway; and Dora, for the Basin and the Casino Pier. Lillian went straight to the Ferris wheel and found out where James was to enlist his help. In minutes James passed the description of Tess to his underground network of people throughout the fairgrounds.

Phoebe ran back to the Children's Building and called upon the next shift of the Broom Brigade. They quit their posts and rushed out after her, still wearing their caps and aprons. They fanned out through the Wooded Island and swarmed around the Fine Arts Building and the states buildings.

Dora stumbled upon Ben, quite by accident, rolling at top speed near the Statue of the Republic. When she told him what the emergency was about, he immediately signaled to every gospel chariot driver he could find to help with the search up and down the lakefront.

Lemonade sellers and spoon peddlers scoured the Midway. Esquimaux abandoned their exhibit and raced around the Battleship Illinois and the Government Plaza still carrying their spears and frightening several ladies from Cincinnati. The startled women assumed some kind of uprising was in progress. Chariot drivers rocketed past the Japanese Tea House, the music stands, and Music Hall. They invaded the Fisheries Building with their empty rolling chairs, determined to make themselves into heroes.

The Broom Brigade swarmed the Wooded Island and the Ho-o-den Temple calling, "Tess! Tess!" in such piercing, high-pitched voices that many visitors assumed they were giving a Japanese language demonstration. The tourists took up the chant, too. The Wooded Island bridges, walkways, and lagoons echoed with "Tess! Tess!"

And still there was no sign of her.

After an hour had passed, Dora dashed back to the Children's Building. She had hoped to see Tess, and she was terribly disappointed. Instead what she discovered was a milling crowd of policemen and Columbian guards and ladies she recognized from the Travelers' Aid Society. In the midst of all the confusion, Dora spotted Ben. A camera flashed. Ben posed. He stood beside his chair, pointing, as if he were directing the whole operation. The valiant gospel chariot driver.

Dora hid behind a Horticulture Building potted plant. She had been tricked. They had all been tricked. As she saw her sisters approach, she desperately signaled to them. Ben was too busy to have noticed Phoebe and Lillian, who scurried to Dora's hiding place. "Hurry!" Dora said. "We have to sneak away before we're recognized."

"I don't know," Phoebe said nervously. "What about Tess? Maybe the police can help us."

"Looks like a trap," said Lillian. She peered around the column. "Ben's the one next to the chair, right? He's talking to somebody with a uniform. There goes James. We lost his help, that's for sure." She folded her arms and made a loud *humph*. "James and the others would have found her, if anybody could. What are we going to do now?"

"Looks hopeless," Phoebe whispered. "They'll call Mama unfit and make us live in some orphanage."

"This is all your fault, Dora," Lillian said, scowling. "We'd never be in this fix if you watched Tess properly."

"*My* fault?" Dora exploded. "What do you know about watching Tess properly? You never help take care of her. Why—"

"That's enough," Phoebe said. "We have to stick together, remember?"

"What are we going to do?" Lillian demanded.

"Follow me," Dora said. She dodged from column to column until they were out of sight of the crowd of officers in front of the Children's Building.

"Where are we going?" Phoebe demanded.

"Streets of Cairo," Dora said. She retraced her steps from the day of her visit to the Midway. The girls dodged past the camel drivers and barkers. They had spent enough time in enough different theaters to know there had to be a back door—a kind of escape hatch. They raced around the line of people, past the sign that said, GENUINE NATIVE MUSCLE DANCE. Dora and her sisters rushed around to the back of the building and tried the door. Amazingly, it opened.

A fat man in a derby tipped back in his chair, reading the newspaper and chomping on a cigar. "What do you think you're doing?" he demanded.

"We're here to see our mother," Dora said sweetly.

"Your mother?"

Before he could haul himself to his feet, the girls had dodged backstage. They could hear the sound of the Zulu band playing, and they followed the eerie noise. There were panels hanging from the ceiling depicting scenes from the Nile.

"This way," Lillian hissed. She expertly followed her nose—the scent of greasepaint meant the dressing room had to be nearby. A small, cramped backstage area with a long mirror lit by lightbulbs revealed ten identical-looking women from the chorus. They all wore the same black shoulder-length wigs cut with severe bangs. Their eyes were painted with wide black lines in the shape of fish. Several of the chorus women were busy putting the final touches on their bright red lips. They all wore the same flimsy costumes.

"Mama?" Phoebe and Lillian called.

The women all looked up at once. "There!" Dora said, pointing.

"What are you doing here?" Mama asked. She sat on the far end with a surprised look on her face. "Did you come to see the show?"

The girls shook their heads.

"No children back here. You know the rules, Melba," another one of the chorus girls said and smacked her lips.

"Tess," Phoebe blurted. "She's missing. We can't find her."

Mama leapt to her feet, knocking over a jar of makeup. She slipped on her golden painted sandals. "Where do you think you're going? We got an act, you know," one of the other chorus girls complained.

"Got to look for my baby," Mama said over her shoulder. She grabbed her pocketbook.

"Two minutes," the stage manager shouted into the costume room. "Hey, where do you think you're going?"

"My daughter's missing."

"You leave, you're fired."

"I quit," Mama said and galloped out the door behind Dora, Lillian, and Phoebe. Dora could hardly believe what Mama had said. Maybe she loved them more than she realized.

Mama dashed through the crowds at the Midway, still wearing her hootchy-kootchy outfit. "Hey, there goes Little Egypt!" someone shouted. "Can I have your autograph?"

It wasn't long before rumors began to fly through the fair. Little Egypt's child had been kidnapped. People who heard this news joined the search. By the time Dora and her sisters and mother arrived back at the Children's Building, an even more enormous crowd had gathered. But as soon as the proper women carrying proper parasols saw Mama, they began to hiss and boo. *"That* is the mother?" the women from the Travelers' Aid Society said in horrified tones. "She's the one who does that awful dance."

"Simply horrid, not a touch of grace in it," another woman in the crowd fumed, "only a most deforming movement of the whole abdominal and lumbar region."

"Indecent," her friend agreed. "Absolutely disgusting."

The men in the crowd seemed very impressed, however.

"Mama!" a voice shouted. Dora and her sisters ran faster. Somewhere in this great milling crowd they heard a wonderful sound. Tess's voice.

"Here she is!" said Miss Rue.

Tess ran through the crowd to embrace Mama. Cameras clicked. Tess hugged her mother so hard that her wig nearly fell off. "Will you look at that?" one of the reporters from the *Chicago Tribune* said admiringly. "A real family moment."

Dora, Phoebe, and Lillian also gave Tess an enormous hug. "Where were you?" Lillian demanded. "What happened?"

"She was inadvertently picked up by the wrong person," Miss Rue explained. She smiled weakly as the cameras flashed again. It seemed everyone in the place was carrying one of the little square Brownie model cameras. "The confusion's been cleared up, however. The nanny brought her back right away when she realized it was the wrong child. She found the little girl she was supposed to be watching. All's well that ends well."

"Can you make a comment about that other kid—Charley?" one of the reporters hollered.

"Hold still," a photographer from another newspaper shouted. "I want to get a picture of the sisters together. Reunited. You get in the picture too, Little Egypt."

Mama grinned from ear to ear. This was exactly the kind of publicity she had always dreamed of. She gathered her daughters around her and beamed. Tess also seemed pleased. She was busy eating the third box of Cracker Jack given to her by several of the policemen.

"Out of my way!" a shrill voice announced. "Stand back! Stand back!" The crowd parted, and there, standing in regal, fuming elegance, was Mrs. Bertha Palmer. "What, may I ask, is this all about? This is unseemly. We do not appreciate such uncouth displays, which clearly belong on the Midway."

"It's all right now, Mrs. Palmer," Miss Rue whispered. "Everything's under control."

"This does nothing for the good name of the Board of Lady Managers. Disperse at once!" She clapped her heavily ringed hands together. Then she nabbed one of the photographers by the lapel of his coat. "And what, may I ask, are you going to do with those pictures? No photos are allowed to be taken on the premises for publicity purposes without the express permission of the Board of Lady Managers."

"I have a permit," the photographer said, wriggling free.

"I can see that you lose your permit. I can see that you lose your job, too. Do I make myself clear?" she replied and gave him a fierce glance. Dutifully, he pulled the film from the back of his camera and handed it to her. Mrs. Palmer then turned to Mama. "I can only hope that our visitors, the thousands of people who come in the Women's Building and the Children's Building every day, do not think that you are representative of our ideal of the kind of mother we are trying to promote."

Mama smiled weakly. Dora held her breath, hoping that for once Mama would keep her mouth shut. "I'd just like to say—" Mama said, her face slightly coloring with anger at the disappearance of her fame as the film was destroyed.

"Silence!" Mrs. Palmer said. "Someone give her a blanket to cover herself. For shame, woman!" A member of the Travelers' Aid Society dashed into the Women's Building and pulled from an exhibit a blanket that had been hand knit by a lady from Oregon. "Here. Not another word."

"Should we have her arrested?" one of the Women's Building officials demanded. She glared at Mama and the girls.

"Officer?" Mrs. Palmer asked. Her voice was less a question than an order.

"Look, Mrs. Palmer. We can't haul somebody away for wearing the wrong outfit," the policeman replied. "I suggest that we just let this here family be on their way. We've had enough excitement here, don't you think, ma'am? Once Little Egypt here leaves the fair—your jurisdiction, so to speak—the newspapers will take over." He winked. "And there won't be nothing you can do about it."

Mrs. Palmer cleared her throat dramatically. "Very well. Be gone, you and your girls," she announced. With a great sweep of her elegant silk cape, Mrs. Palmer left the scene.

Gratefully, Dora and her sisters and mother decided to hurry home to the dormitory. They had some rather strange looks on the trolley. For once Mama did not seem to notice. She held Tess on her lap the whole way. Dora glanced around the car at the other passengers. Even though some people were making disapproving *tsk tsk* noises, Dora didn't care. She felt too happy.

"You quit your job," Lillian said as they walked up the dormitory front steps. "I can't believe you quit."

"Something will turn up," Mama said. "Something always turns up. Don't worry." She gave Tess a tender pat and set her down on the ground. "First thing I'm going to do is get rid of this ugly blanket. Can you imagine somebody thought this was attractive? The women in Oregon must have no taste at all."

"Hello," a voice called.

Mama looked up. So did Dora and her sisters. Standing beside the front door was Da. Behind him, staring out from the screen door, were the ladies from the Women's Dormitory Association.

"Da!" the girls cried and rushed to him. He gathered them in his arms and swung them round and round on the porch.

"Goodness!" said one of the spinsters, who was perched in a rocking chair.

"Will you look at that! Wonderful!" another replied.

"I've been waiting and waiting for you," Da said. "How come you never answered my notes? How come you never told me what was going on?" he demanded. "I've been worried sick. Each time I've come here for you, they send me away. No men, they say. I leave notes. You don't answer. This is my first day off since I started. Melba, I've been sitting here waiting for you to come back since morning."

For once, Mama couldn't seem to find any words. She was stunned.

"What show you in?" Da asked, inspecting Mama's wig.

"It's a long, long story," Mama replied in a tired voice.

Dora and her sisters were delighted to see Da. They could scarcely believe he had returned for them. They weren't abandoned after all.

"When do we see the Wild West Show?" Tess demanded.

Da laughed. "Soon as you like." He looked tired and much older than Dora remembered.

That very evening, as soon as Mama had removed her black wig and makeup, they went to the Wild West Show. It was even more marvelous than Dora or her sisters thought it would be. They cheered to see the cowboys, Indians, Cossacks, Mexicans, and Arabs on horseback tear around the amphitheater area. Annie Oakley shot at clay pigeons sprung from a trap. The Pony Express delivered the mail. A covered wagon was attacked by Indians and chased away by Buffalo Bill himself and a group of cowboys. Then the Deadwood mail coach was ambushed and rescued by Buffalo Bill. Best of all was the buffalo hunt, the last of the only known native herd.

Dora and her sisters watched nervously as the shaggy creatures galloped around and around. No one actually shot them, Phoebe was relieved to discover. "It's pretend," she shouted to Dora.

"Of course," Lillian replied in a superior voice. "Buffaloes are nearly extincted."

Extinct was a spelling word Dora remembered. For once she didn't try to correct Lillian. She simply enjoyed the evening. She looked around at her parents and her sisters. They were together again. And that was better than any wild bareback race or thrilling bucking bronco demonstration. Better even than watching handsome Buffalo Bill riding full gallop, long hair streaming, as he blasted a ball thrown in midair with his trusty Winchester.

Chapter 12

"Why can't we go?" Lillian whined. It was a fine, sunny day in early October. She sat in the dormitory window and looked out at the steady stream of people rushing down Ellis Avenue toward the Chicago Day festivities at the fairgrounds.

"Too dangerous," Dora said. She intended to keep a careful eye on her sisters. What would it matter if they stayed away one day from their jobs in the Children's Building? "Never saw so many people in all my life. Someone's going to get hurt."

"We're missing everything," Phoebe said, pouting. "The parade's going to have floats, brass bands. I heard they're letting children march in colorful costumes and carry banners and flags. And what about the fireworks out on the lake?"

Dora didn't care. She wasn't taking any chances. Chicago Day sounded like bad luck to her. The celebration was supposed to commemorate the Great Fire of 1871 that started when Mrs. O'Leary's cow kicked over a lantern and set off a blaze that destroyed nearly the entire city. Why would anyone want to have a celebration for such a disaster?

For the rest of the afternoon, Dora and her sisters tried to amuse themselves in the dormitory. Tess doctored Nancy, the invalid. Lillian invented new dance routines. Dora reread the tattered dormitory library copy of *Mill on the Floss*. Phoebe scribbled postcards to Florence. One said:

> Deer Florence:
> Like this prety card?
> Good news Charley got a new fambly
> he left Nursry we miss him but
> I no hes happy Mama is working at
> the Colnyal Exibyt. She gets to
> ware a costum and act oldfashnd so
> she is happy to she talks but she cant dance
> once she sang peeple clapped
> Da says we leev soon as the Wild West Show
> closes He says he's sick and tired

of the Big city we're going
to try Manitoo Springs this time
— Phoebe

Later, when Mama returned very late she said she
had never seen such a mob. "Nearly a million, they
say," Mama said in a weary voice. "The sea of trash
they left behind was unbelievable. You could hardly
walk without stepping on something—lost over-
coats, table casters, fur shoulder capes. Heaps of cat-
alogs, umbrellas, and souvenir badges. Enough odd
gloves to sink a ship. I waded knee-deep in guide
books, tobacco pouches, canes, straw hats, and
satchels. Even saw a pug dog running around lost."

"We could use a dog," Lillian said.

Mama sighed. "Don't start." She lay on the bed
with her shoes still on her feet.

"Want me to fix you something to eat?" Phoebe
asked.

Mama shook her head. "No thanks, darling.
You go on back to sleep."

The next day Dora and her sisters read in the
newspaper that five people had been killed and
nearly twenty-four others injured in the traffic and
reckless mobs that had roamed Chicago Day. In
the first hour, nearly 16,000 people had jammed
the Casino Pier and overwhelmed the Movable

Sidewalk. "See?" Dora said triumphantly. "I was right. It was a good thing we didn't go."

But her sisters were not satisfied. They did not want to be safe. They wanted to be thrilled and entertained.

The weather in October turned cold and raw. Lake wind whistled through the cracks in the warped pine dormitory walls. The girls shivered when they jumped out of bed in the morning. School had started in many places, and the school-teachers and many of the dormitory's other guests packed up and left. Soon Mama, Dora, and her sisters were among the last remaining tenants. The dormitory filled with echoes as the girls rambled carelessly down the long hallways. They could sing and jump and holler as much as they wanted because their neighbors were all gone.

"Not so much fun making a racket when there's nobody to tell you to be quiet," Lillian said sadly. She and Phoebe missed Miss Shattuck, who had left for South Dakota.

With so many children back in school, the Broom Brigade was disbanded. The gymnasium closed down. The nursery shut its doors. Even James and his gang moved off the grounds. The pickings were just too slim at that point. Ben and the other chair pushers drifted off to start college again. Dora never said good-bye to him. She was still too angry about his betrayal. Even so, she would have liked to see him wink at her one last time. She wished she were lucky enough to be going back to school.

One windy, gray afternoon in late October, Dora and her sisters went back to visit the White City for the last time. The next day they were leaving Chicago with their parents and heading west on a train for Colorado. As they walked among the skull-white buildings, they noticed places where cracked plaster had flaked away like dead skin. The buildings were unheated and as insubstantial as stage scenery. Phoebe found this discovery most distressing. She wanted to believe that the White City could not crumble. She wanted to believe that it had been built to last for centuries.

Lillian could not look at the silent, motionless Ferris wheel without feeling sad. The Ferris wheel, operated only on weekends now, seemed as if it had been misplaced by some giant. A lost toy hoop.

Out on the lake and the lagoons, there were no boats. "Don't hear any barkers on the Midway," Dora said, "no music, no voices." The fairgrounds had become as forlorn and deserted as a tomb.

Tess glanced warily up at the huge, somber statues whose faces were so far away it hurt her neck to try and look at them. When she noticed their enormous eyes, she felt so afraid that the hair on the back of her neck stood straight up. She looked away and tried hard not to think that the heavy-bodied statues with heads as big as baby carriages, chimney-sized arms, and legs stouter than trees might be watching her and her sisters. "Good-bye, Chicago!" Tess hollered as bravely as she could. Her voice echoed among the motionless angels and warriors and famous explorers.

The girls watched men rolling carts with huge crates to the Fine Arts Building. Soon they would begin removing paintings, sculptures, and murals. "I'll never see so many elegant paintings again," Lillian said with a dramatic sigh. "I'm afraid everything will seem small and dull after this."

Phoebe nodded. "I can't believe it's going to end."

The girls walked past the Horticulture Building. Wind skittered old newspapers and wrappers across the lagoon. Dead leaves tumbled into neglected corners. Out on Wooded Island, the trees stood gaunt and bare. Dora held her elbows close and peered at the deserted island. "Remember the fireworks out there? Remember all the people?"

"Such a pity this beauty will soon be gone," Lillian agreed. "Like waking up from an enchanted dream."

Soft rain fell. The girls hurried. Tess waved to the familiar elk that flanked the Columbian Fountain. They watched spray fall on statues of struggling horses and awkward riders. High atop the boat in an uncomfortable chair rode Mrs. Columbia. She did not seem to notice the wind and rain in her face.

"Make a wish," Lillian said and handed each of her sisters a shiny penny. For once, even Tess cooperated. She seemed to sense that something serious was about to happen. With precision she copied her sisters. The girls turned so that their backs faced the fountain. They tossed their pennies one by one over their right shoulders. *Plunk plunk plunk plunk.*

"Tell your wish, Dorie," Tess insisted.

Dora shook her head. "Won't come true if I don't keep it secret."

Lillian noticed Dora's grin. "Manitou might be the place. The big break," Lillian said in her best, ever-hopeful voice.

"Something will turn up," Phoebe and Dora replied. They laughed, linked little fingers, and turned around twice for speaking the same words at the same time.

"Come on." Dora motioned for the girls to follow. She knew they had a lot to do before their long journey tomorrow. Da was going to meet them at the dormitory and help Mama pack.

The girls walked for the last time out the main gate. Dora paused at that moment. She knew she could never return. The fair was about to vanish forever.

"You sick, Dora?" Lillian demanded.

Dora shook her head. How could she explain? No matter what happened next to her family, she and her sisters would need to remember this special place, this special time. How they rescued each other. How they never gave up. It was a story to give them courage, to keep them whole.

Dora needn't have worried that her sisters might forget. Even before Lillian, Phoebe, and Tess reached Fifty-sixth Street, they turned to Dora and demanded, "Tell it again."

"Which part?"

"Everything."

Bibliography

PRIMARY SOURCES

Allensworth, Emma H. Diary, July 1893, Manuscript, Southern Historical Collection, University of North Carolina at Chapel Hill, NC.

Cotten, Sallie Southall. Diary, May-November 1893, Manuscript, Southern Historical Collection, University of North Carolina at Chapel Hill, NC.

SECONDARY SOURCES

Applebaum, Stanley. *The Chicago World's Fair of 1893.* NY: Dover Publications, Inc., 1980.

Badger, R. Reid. *The Great American Fair.* Chicago: Nelson Hall, 1979.

Brown, Dee. *Hear that Lonesome Whistle Blow:*

Railroads in the West. NY: Touchstone, Simon & Schuster, 1977.

Burg, David F. *Chicago's White City of 1893.* Lexington: University Press of Kentucky, 1976.

Cronon, William. *Nature's Metropolis, Chicago and the Great West.* NY: W. W. Norton, 1991.

Duis, Perry R. *Challenging Chicago: Coping with Everyday Life, 1837-1920.* Chicago: University of Urbana Press, 1998.

Harris, Neil, editor. *Grand Illusions: Chicago's World's Fair of 1893.* Chicago: Chicago Historical Society, 1993.

Johnson, Rossiter, editor. *A History of the World's Columbian Exposition,* Vol. 1-4. NY: D. Appleton and Company, 1897.

Muccigrosso, Robert. *Celebrating the New World: Chicago's Columbian Exposition of 1893.* Chicago: Ivan R. Dee, 1993.

Rosa, Joseph G., and Robin May. *Buffalo Bill and His Wild West.* Lawrence, KS: University of Kansas Press, 1989.

Spinney, Robert G. *City of Big Shoulders: A History of Chicago.* DeKalb, IL: Northern Illinois University Press, 2000.

Swanson, Stevenson. *Chicago Days.* Chicago: Contemporary Books, 1997.

Weimann, Jeanne Madeline. *The Fair Women: The Story of the Woman's Building.* Chicago: Academy Chicago, 1981.

About the Author

Trained as a journalist, Laurie Lawlor worked for many years as a freelance writer and editor before devoting herself full-time to the creation of children's books. She enjoys many speaking engagements at schools and libraries, and her books have been nominated for many awards. She lives in Evanston, Illinois, with her husband, son, daughter, and two large Labrador retrievers. Her books include the *Addie Across the Prairie* series, the *Heartland* series, *How to Survive Third Grade*, *The Worm Club*, *Gold in the Hills*, and *Little Women* (a movie novelization). Her nonfiction work, *Shadow Catcher: The Life and Work of Edward S. Curtis*, won the Carl Sandburg Award for nonfiction (1995) and the Golden Kite Honor Book Award (1995).